THE BOY SCOUTS IN FRONT OF WARSAW

OR

IN THE WAKE OF WAR

GEORGE DURSTON

1st WORLD
LIBRARY
Literary Society

The Boy Scouts in Front of Warsaw

George Durston

© 1st World Library – Literary Society, 2005
PO Box 2211
Fairfield, IA 52556
www.1stworldlibrary.org
First Edition

LCCN: 2005906477

Softcover ISBN: 1-4218-1533-8
Hardcover ISBN: 1-4218-1433-1
eBook ISBN: 1-4218-1633-4

Purchase *"The Boy Scouts in Front of Warsaw"*
as a traditional bound book at:
www.1stWorldLibrary.org/purchase.asp?ISBN=1-4218-1533-8

1st World Library Literary Society is a nonprofit
organization dedicated to promoting literacy by:

- Creating a free internet library accessible from any
  computer worldwide.
- Hosting writing competitions and offering book
  publishing scholarships.

Readers interested in supporting literacy
through sponsorship, donations or
membership please contact:
literacy@1stworldlibrary.org
Check us out at: www.1stworldlibrary.ORG
and start downloading free ebooks today.

The Boy Scouts in Front of Warsaw
contributed by Tim, Ed & Rodney
in support of
1st World Library Literary Society

CHAPTER I

THE DISAPPEARANCE

It was the fifth of August. Warsaw the brilliant, Warsaw the Beautiful, the best beloved of her adoring people, had fallen. Torn by bombs, wrecked by great shells, devastated by hordes of alien invaders, she lay in ruins.

Her people, despairing, seemed for the greater part to have vanished in the two days since the fatal third of August when the city was taken.

Many of the wealthiest of her citizens had taken refuge in the lower part of the city, leaving their magnificent palaces and residences situated in the newer part to the flood of invading soldiers, who went with unerring directness to the parts containing the greatest comfort and luxury.

Warsaw is built in the midst of a beautiful plain mostly on the left bank of the river Vistula. All the main part of the city lies close to the river, and the streets are so twisted and crooked that it is almost impossible to picture them. They wriggle here and there like snakes of streets. The houses, of course, are very old, and with their heavy barred doors and solid shutters, look very strange and inhospitable.

People, in a way, become like their surroundings. Here in these twisted, narrow streets are to be found the narrow, twisted souls of the worst element in Poland; but the worst of them love their country as perhaps no other people do. To the last man and to the frailest woman, they are loyal to Poland. For them, it is Poland first, last and always.

In these low and twisted streets, the devastation was greatest and the people had scurried like rats to cover. A week before they had swarmed the streets and crowded the buildings. Now by some miracle they had gone, utterly disappeared. The houses were deserted, the streets empty. The destruction had been greatest in these crowded places, but many of the beautiful public buildings and state departments in the new part were also in ruins, as well as a number of matchless palaces.

The people from the upper part of the city who had taken refuge in the holes along the river front, were for the most part a strange appearing lot. Some of them carried great bundles which they guarded with jealous care. Others, empty handed, sat and shivered through the summer night-chills that blew from the river. Scores of little children clung to their mother's hands, or wandered trembling and screaming from group to group, seeking their own people.

There was a general gathering of types. Nobles mixed with the poorest, meanest and most criminal classes, and mingled with their common sorrow. For the most part a dumbness, a silence prevailed. The shock of the national disaster had bereft the people of their powers of expression.

Since 1770, Poland had been torn and racked by foes on every hand. Prussia, Austria and Russia envied her wealth, courage, and her fertile plains. Little by little her enemies had pressed across her shrinking borders, wet with the blood of her patriot sons. Little by little she had lost her cherished land until the day of doom August third, 1915.

Sitting, hiding in their desolated city, the people of Poland knew that theirs was a country no longer on the map. Russia, Austria and Prussia at least had met. There was no longer any

Poland. For generations there had been no Polish language; it was forbidden by her oppressors. Now the country itself was swallowed up. No longer on the changing map of the world had she any place.

But in the hearts of her people Poland lives. With the most perfect loyalty and love in the world, they say, "We are Poland. We live and die for her."

A gray haze hung over Warsaw. The streets, after the roar of great guns, the bursting of shells, and the cries of thousands of people rushing blindly to safety, seemed silent and deserted. The hated enemy held the town, and the people of Warsaw, most hapless city of all history, cowered beneath the iron hand of the enemy.

As is usual in the fearful lull after such a victory, the town was filled with dangers of the most horrible sort. Murder, crime of every kind, lawlessness in every guise, stalked through the streets or lurked down the narrow, dark and twisted alleys. The unfortunate citizens who had not retreated in time hid, when they could, in all sorts of strange places. They gathered in trembling, whispering groups, into garrets and cellars; even the vaults in the catacombs, the old burial place of the dead, were opened by desperate fugitives, and became hiding places for the living.

The soldiers were in possession of all the uninjured residences in the more modern portion of the city, where they reveled in the comforts of modern baths, lights and heat. But the lower part of the city, lying along the left bank of the river Vistula, was filled with a strange mixture of terrified people. In all the throngs, huddled in streets and alleys, storehouses and ware-rooms, there was perhaps no stranger group than the one gathered in a dark corner of a great building where machinery of some sort had been manufactured.

This had, strangely enough, escaped destruction and stood unharmed in a street where everything bore the scars of shells or bombs.

The engines were stopped; the great wheels motionless; the broad belts sagged hopelessly. Even the machinery seemed to feel the terrible blow and mourned the fallen city.

The persons huddled in the shadow of a vast wheel, however, gave little heed to their strange surroundings. They seemed crushed by a frightful grief more personal even than the taking of Warsaw would cause in the most loyal heart.

In the center of the group a boy of fourteen or fifteen years stood talking excitedly. He was tall, dark as an Italian, and dressed with the greatest richness. Two rings set with great jewels flashed on his hand and while he spoke, he tapped his polished boot with a small cane in the end of which was set a huge, sparkling red stone. He spoke with great rapidity, in the pure Russian of the Court, and addressed himself to an elderly man who sat drooping in an attitude of hopeless sorrow.

Near them sat a plainly dressed woman who buried her stained face in her apron, and wept the hard sobs of those who can scarcely weep more. A young girl clung to her, silent but with beautiful dark eyes wild with terror and loss. On the floor lay a wounded soldier, bearing in perfect silence the frightful pain of a shattered shoulder. His only bandage was a piece of cloth wound tightly around his coat, but not a groan escaped his pale lips. At the window, gazing down into the wrecked street, stood a tall boy of perhaps fifteen years. His face was bloodless; his strong mouth was set in a straight line; the hand resting on the window sill was clenched until the knuckles shone white through the tanned skin. Desperation, horror, and grief struggled equally in his face. His left arm encircled a boy nearly his own size. He, like the woman, sobbed brokenly, and the taller boy patted him as he listened to the rapid words of the boy who was talking.

Suddenly the elderly man spoke.

"You must pardon me, Ivanovich," he said in a trembling voice. "I do not seen to comprehend. Will you kindly repeat your account?"

A flash of anger passed over the face of the young nobleman; then he spoke courteously.

"Certainly, Professor! It was thus. You remember, don't you, that I came to your house as usual, five days ago, for my lessons in English? And you know the sudden bombardment, so close to the city, was so terrible that you would not let me go home? Good! Then you understand all, up to this morning. You know we had watched all night with the doors barricaded, and we decided it was too unsafe to remain longer in the direct path of those brutal soldiers. So we prepared to come here, to one of my father's buildings where there is a chute and an underground storeroom where we could be safe.

"You send me for this cloak and when I returned, what did I find in the room where I had left everyone of the household gathered ready for the flight? The room was empty. I had been upstairs perhaps ten minutes because I could not find my cloak, and there was the room empty. Sir, I was furious at you for leaving me. I am in your charge; I am a Prince; yet you left me - "

The tall boy turned from the window and spoke.

"Never mind that, Ivan," he said. "Just cut that all out and hustle to the part you haven't told." Although he spoke English, while Ivan told his story in Russian, the boys understood each other perfectly for with a frown and quick glance, the boy Ivan nodded and continued.

"I stood for a while and listened but heard nothing. Then I went through the other rooms on the floor, and all were empty. I decided to get to the warehouse alone if I could, and crept to the door. I drew back hastily. A horrible old woman squatted on the step. She was watching over two great sacks full, no doubt, of valuables stolen from your house and others. As I looked, two men came up. Criminals, they looked, and I scarcely breathed. Presently they went away, the men throwing the sacks over their shoulders, and the woman dragging a jeweled Icon in her hand.

"I heard footsteps behind me, and there you were coming down the stairs. You had that package in your hands, and you said, 'Just think, I nearly forgot my book, Ivan; my great book on the history of Warsaw, now so nearly finished.'

"You asked where the others were, and you said they had thought it wise to go in two parties. You said they had told you to be very careful of something; you couldn't very well remember just what, but it made you remember your book in your and you hurried to save it. So we hurried out, and managed to escape the soldiers, and get here and then everyone cried out, 'Where are the children?'"

"When I went to get my book," said the Professor, with a groan, "they were sitting quiet as mice by the stove, holding each other's hands. How could they have gone off?"

The woman looked up. "They could not go," she said. "I myself slid the great latch on the door; they could not lift it. I have seen Elinor try to do so. The little stranger was much too small. The Germans have them, I am sure of it." She bowed her head with fresh sobs.

"There were no Germans about," said Ivan. "No soldiers of any sort; no one at all save the three of whom I spoke and they certainly did not take them away."

"Certainly not!" said Professor Morris, frowning. "They must have gone out and wandered off while I was after my book, although I distinctly told Elinor not to stir from her seat. I have always endeavored to teach my children absolute obedience. I am surprised at Elinor. She understood. She is six years of age, and she said, "Yes, father.""

This is a terrible thing; but they will be found. I will report at once to the military authorities. I am convinced that they are safe. Someone will take them in just as we took in the strange child whom we found at the door. That child, as you know, is a noble, yet she was lost. These are war times. People are glad to return lost children. They do not want them. Now if I had forgotten my book, it might have been burned; three years of effort in this city wasted and lost forever! I will hide the manuscript in the underground room you told of, Ivan, then we will go to the proper authorities, and get the children."

"Bah!" said the soldier with the broken shoulder suddenly. "Go where thou wilt these days there is no authority save the authority of brute might. Will that help thee?"

"We must find them," said the Professor brokenly. The seriousness of the affair was beginning to dawn on him. "It will certainly be simple. We will advertise."

The girl at his side smiled. "Advertise?" she said. "Why, father, there are no papers left to advertise in."

"Ivan," said the tall boy at the window, "did you hear what the three people at the door were talking about? What did they say? The people you said looked like thieves."

"Yes, they talked," said Ivan, "but it did not seem to mean much. I didn't get much from it anyway."

"Try to think what they said," said the boy. He passed a hand carefully across the bright fairness of his hair where a dark red streak stained it. "Can't you remember anything they said?"

Ivan stood thinking, the jeweled cane still tapping his boot. "Yes," he said, "when the men came up, they said, 'What have you?' The woman laughed - evilly, and said, 'All the wine we can drink, and all the bread we can eat, and all the fire we burn for years and years.'"

"The man who had spoken said 'Jewels,' and rubbed his hands. 'That is indeed good! Jewels fit for a king!"

"The woman said, "Jewels now, thou fool! Where can one sell jewels these days when one cannot cross the border, and when the world cracks? No one wants jewels!"

"'Then what?' said the man.

"'Oh, stupid!' said the woman. 'Pick up my sacks carefully and be off."

"Then the other man who had already picked up the larger sack, laughed. 'Better than rubies," he said. 'You are always wise, my woman!"

"And then the other man picked up the other sack and he laughed too, and the woman held hand to them and whined, 'Please give me some money for these poor little refugees are starving!'

"At that they all roared, and hurried on."

Ivan paused. "That was all they said," he added. "It doesn't help, does it?"

The girl Evelyn leaned forward. "Say it again, Ivan," she said excitedly. "Say just what the woman said"

Ivan, repeated the words.

Evelyn whispered them after him. Then a wild cry broke from her lips. She turned to her father who sat holding the package containing the fatal manuscript. She seized his arm and shook him. So great was her emotion that she could not say the words she wanted.

"Father, father, don't you see it now!" she cried. "Oh, oh, father! Oh, what shall we do? Oh, my darling little sister!" she gasped, and the tall boy ran forward and seized her hands.

"Control yourself, Evelyn," he cried. "I never saw you act like this. Tell me what it is."

She looked at him quite speechless. The agony of all that she had witnessed, the terror of the past week, the fright of losing her precious little sister scarcely more than a baby, the blindness of her father, all had combined to send her into state scarcely better than insanity. With a desperate effort to control, herself, she looked into her brother's eyes.

"You see, don't you, Warren?" she begged. "You can't seem to be able say it.

Say you see it too, Warren!"

Then as if she had found some way of giving him her message of doom, she drooped against brother's strong shoulder and fainted quietly away. Warren laid her down, and the governess rushed to her.

"Is she dead?" asked Warren.

"Certainly not," said the woman; "she has fainted."

"What did she try to tell you?" cried Ivan. "Was it something I said?"

"Yes, you told her," said Warren, "and she read it right. I know she is right."

"Well, well, what is it?" demanded the Professor. "This is fearfully upsetting, fearfully upsetting!"

Warren bent tenderly above his sister. She was regaining consciousness.

"It is about as bad as it can be," he said hesitatingly. "The remark about refugees told the whole thing. Our little sister was in one of those sacks, gagged or unconscious. They have been stolen to be used and brought up as beggars."

A deep silence followed. The governess covered her eyes. The wounded soldier slowly shook his head. Professor Morris, Ivan and jack stood with bulging eyes staring at Warren, trying to make themselves understand his speech. Ivan, who knew more of the ways of the half barbaric people of Poland and Russia, nodded his head understandingly. Jack stood with open mouth. The Professor rumpled his hair, though deeply, and laughed.

"Now what would they do that for!" he asked sarcastically. "That sort of thing is not done nowadays."

"Not in the best families," said Warren coldly. "But it is done, I'll bet."

"Oh, yes, it's done," said Ivan, "all the time. I know my father talked a lot about it just before the commencement of the war. He was going to try to stamp out a lot of that sort of thing, especially what affected the women and children. Yes, it is done, Professor."

"Not now," said the Professor stubbornly. "There was recorded a case of that sort in 1793, and even later in the early sixties. Later, there are no records at all bearing on the subject. And if no records, surely there are no instances requiring the attention of thinking people.

"It would be most natural to record any instance of the sort, however small and trifling. In my researches I would have run across the facts. There is no mention of it whatever."

"I know it happens anyhow," said Ivan, sticking to his point.

"Ivan, you forget that I am in a position to know," said the Professor. "My researches have led me, thanks to the presentations of your father and many others, into secret records never before opened to outsiders of any race. I regret the stand you take with me. I am unused to contradiction."

"Pardon me," said Ivan wearily. He looked at Warren. In the minds of both boys there was a feeling that the mystery was solved. There was no longer any need to discuss it. A little search around the house would show if the children were there; after that it meant that Evelyn was right.

"Well, Ivan's right," said Warren doggedly. "It doesn't matter what you have found in your researches, father; you have had those dry old records to prove everything to you. I have heard the people tell stories that would make your hair curl. They not only steal children, but sometimes they cripple them, just as they did hundreds of years ago in England. Why do you suppose boys like Ivan here are watched every second? Sometimes they take them for revenge, but when they are gone, they are gone. You can't go out with a wad of bills and stick it under the park fence, and go back and find your child on the front stoop like you can at home."

CHAPTER II

THE SEARCH BEGUN

"Impossible!" said the Professor. "Impossible, Warren! It surprises me that you should harbor such wild and impracticable ideas."

"It makes sound sense, dad," said Warren sadly. "Europe has been full of beggars from the beginning of time. And soon, after the war is over, there will be thousands of sightseers flooding the continent. What could be more practical from the standpoint of such people as the ones described by Ivan than to secure two beautiful little children like our Elinor and the strange child that wandered to our doors? They would indeed mean 'drink and money and fire.'" He stopped and for a moment looked reproachfully at his father. "Oh, father, father," he cried, "see what your dreadful forgetfulness has done! How will you ever forgive yourself when you think of the misery and suffering you have brought on your darling! I can scarcely forgive you."

Professor Morris sat with bowed head.

"My son," he said brokenly, "I can not forgive myself. I do not know what to do. I confess I did indeed leave the children. I thought of my book. I thought they were safe - and my book - Warren, surely you do not blame me for getting my book?" He spoke tenderly, even lovingly, and clasped the bulky parcel to his breast.

"No, I do not blame you for anything, father, knowing you as well as I do. It is a terrible thing, but we will find her, our precious darling, if we spend our lives hunting." He turned to his sister and brother. "Won't we?" he said.

They did not reply, but gazed at him with looks that were more than promises.

"Well," he continued, "I guess my boyhood is over now. My work is cut out for me. Come on, Ivan, come Jack, let's get going!"

"What do you think you are going to do, Ivanovich?" asked the wounded soldier. Like all his class, generations of submission made him ignore as much as possible all save the one noble. All his attention was given to Ivan, the young Prince.

"Be careful, Ivanovich," he urged. "It is not possible for you to go forth in the clothes you wear. There is danger lurking abroad for the high born."

Ivan shrugged his fearless shoulders. "They would not dare to harm me," he answered.

"He's right. Those clothes won't do," said Warren decidedly. "We don't know where we are going, nor whom we may meet. Where can we find something rough for you to wear?"

"Down below are the workmen's extra blouses," said the soldier. "When I worked here, the room was kept locked, but you might perhaps force the door. There are blouses and rough shoes there. But I tremble; I tremble!" He suddenly lapsed into Polish. "Let these Americans go, Prince," he begged. "Harm never come to them. They go always as though they wore a charm. Poland shall yet rise, my Prince. From these ashes she shall arise more beautiful than ever. She will need you then."

Ivan listened with flashing eyes. "I shall be here," he said simply. "I shall be here, I shall answer when she calls, but in the meantime shall it be said that in Poland, even in her darkest hour, children were stolen for such evil purposes? Never, never!" He turned to Warren. "For a year now," he said, "we have been organizing these Boy Scouts that you have so many of in America. Let us pass the word to them. If little Elinor and the stranger are to be found, surely they will find them. My rank has always hampered me, but even then I know that boys will go where no others can penetrate. What do you think?"

"It's the dandiest idea I ever heard!" exclaimed Warren, his face lighting. "We will have to depend on passing the word to them as we find them here and there, but it's the only thing to do, so let's go to it."

"First the workman's clothes," said Ivan.

"Assuredly!" exclaimed the Professor. "Let us disguise ourselves and go forth. I know that we will find the dear children playing near the corner."

"Father, you must stay here," said Warren, determination in his voice.

"Of course not; of course not!" said the Professor. "Do you expect me to sit idly here while my youngest child needs my protection?"

A smile as sad as tears crossed Evelyn's pale face. "You must stay here, father," she said. "You would certainly get lost, and then we would have to hunt for you. It has happened so before, you know."

"That was very different," said the Professor. "A man uses all his powers of concentration at times, and if it has happened that I have occasionally been so intent on my studies of Warsaw's past history that I have for the time forgotten my surroundings, it is scarcely to be wondered at. The present occasion is different. You will need a man, with a man's wisdom, and a man's ability to act quickly. I must go; I am ready."

Warren, knowing his father's stubbornness, hesitated. Catching his sister's eye, she shook her head slightly. Professor Morris was scrambling to his feet, still clasping his book.

Warren led his father around the narrow aisle that ran between the great machines, until they were alone. Then he spoke.

"Father," he said, "you cannot go. Today has made a man of me. I am sorry, father, but we children are the ones who are always the victims of your forgetfulness, and we have suffered many times before today. This is the worst of all. Perhaps we shall never see our little Elinor again; and I am the one who promised mother when she died that I would always look out for her. It is my fault that she is lost. I should have known better than to have left her with you, but I meant to see the others safely here, and get back before you started.

"I know you, father; you mean to do the right thing by us always, but I certainly don't know what would happen if we did not look out for you as well as ourselves." His voice trembled. "I know this does not sound like proper talk from a boy to his father; but I've got to say it for once. I promise that I'll never speak so to you again, but I'm going to get it out of my system this time. Since I can remember we have been looking out for you. We have had to take care of you and help you remember your meal times, and your rubbers, and your hat, and overcoat and gloves and necktie. We have had to see that you went to bed, and ate and got up and everything else. And all because of books. It makes you sore at me because I hate them. I ought to hate them! Your writing and reading and studying have been the curse of our lives. I tell you, father, it has been just as bad as any other bad habit or appetite. Why, when you are reading up for some article or digging into some musty old work, you are dead to everything else. And we have had to suffer for it. Do you think any other man you know would have left those children a minute in a time like this?"

He paused and once more pressed a hand carefully on the red stain across his fair hair.

"Oh, you must forgive me for talking so, dad, but I'm pretty sore. Little Elinor - " He turned sharply, and hurried away to Ivan. The three boys hurried down the steep stairs and disappeared. Professor Morris for a moment, a long, dazed moment, stood looking blankly at the dark doorway through which his son had disappeared. Then he sank weakly down on a bench.

As a boy and as a man, he had been noted for his ability to memorize remarks.

In college the worst of the lectures, no matter how dry, had been all imprinted on his mind. Now as he sat thinking, he could fairly see his son's accusing words like large print before his eyes.

For once in his life Benjamin Morris had heard the plain truth from the lips of his favorite son. Yet he did not realize the seriousness of his son's charge. He had heard the words, but their real meaning did not seem to pierce his brain, so filled with knowledge that there was no room there for any interest in the living, or any thought that the present, the passing moment in which we make our little life history, is more precious to each of us then the great moments of the past, no matter how filled they may be with heroic figures.

Benjamin Morris had been long years ago an infant Prodigy. Perhaps you fellows who read this have never known one; and if so, you are lucky. An infant Prodigy shows an unnatural amount of intelligence at a very early age. So far it is all right; and if he belongs to a sensible family, he is urged into athletics, and sleeps out of door and manages to grow up so he will pass in a crowd. But sometimes there are proud parents who read too many books on how to train a child, and pay too little attention to the child himself; and there are aunts, perhaps, as well; and they all take the poor little genius and proceed to train him all out of shape. He rattles off all sorts of pieces, Horatio at the Bridge, and Casabianca, and Anthony's Oration Over Caesar, are easy as pancakes and syrup to him. Then he skips whole grades in school and plows through college like a mole under a rose bush, enjoying himself immensely, no doubt, down there in the dark, but missing all the benefit of the light and air and sunshine. So the infant Prodigy gets to be a grown Prodigy, and presently an old Prodigy, never once suspecting that knowledge, hurtfully taken and wrongfully used, can be almost as great a sin as ignorance.

Certainly Professor Morris, whose sins of learning were heavy ones and bore cruelly on those who loved him in spite of his strange ways, would never have believed any of this. At home, as a boy, when Benny studied, the house was kept so still that incautious mice sometimes came out of their holes and nibbled in broad daylight. At college his queerness, forgetfulness and oddity was excused because of his wonderful recitations and amazing marks. You just couldn't rag a fellow who made one hundred right along. When he married, he found a lovely, gentle girl, who believed him the greatest of all men and held his position as Professor of Ancient History in Princeton as the highest of all earthly positions. But when Elinor was a year old, the little wife died, quite worn out from looking after Professor Benjamin Mollingfort Morris, who had proved to be her most helpless and troublesome child.

Mrs. Morris died warning her older children to look out for the father, and so passed her burden on to them. But some way or other, there was different stuff in the children. They did look after their father, and took good care of the old Prodigy, but the task did not wear them out. Young Jack was indeed so bright that it rather worried Evelyn and Warren, who were always on the alert to overcome any symptoms of genius in themselves or the other children; but owing to their caution, he seemed to be developing well. And Professor Morris, blind to it all, forever digging in the dust of ages, knew nothing of the fact that he was the father of four wonderful children who were successfully carrying on the difficult business of growing up, managing a house, taking care of a parent, and looking after money matters as well.

Warren was the soul of honor. He hated school, but went without a skip, because it was right. And that's a hard thing to do. He looked clean, and was clean, and thought clean. And that's hard, too.

Professor Morris, sitting in his study feverishly seeking facts concerning the table manners of Noah's second cousin twice removed, was deaf and dumb and blind. Yet when he occasionally "came up for air" as Warren put it, the children thought him the finest and funniest and kindest of fathers. It was at one of these times that he came home with the news that he had been given a vacation for three years with full pay. This was to make it possible for him to go to Warsaw, and write an account of some parts of the city's history of which rather little was known.

Warren and Evelyn, who had read "Thaddeus of Warsaw" were wild with delight. It was a glorious journey and, on shipboard at least, it was easy to keep track of the Professor, who had found a very learned Englishman who disagreed with him on every known point. The two old men hurried to find each other each morning, and were dragged apart at night; and the children had time to enjoy the voyage and make many friends. In Warsaw, which they reached safely, they took a house near the magnificent Casimr Palace which now houses the University. Professor Morris did find time to secure fine teachers for the children, and reliable servants for the house. Warren, who always boiled with activity, soon made scores of pals, and immediately introduced the Boy Scouts to Poland.

The young Polish and Russian boys took up the work with the greatest enthusiasm, and time slipped happily away, until war swept the continent. Professor Morris refused to believe in its nearness until it was too late to escape, and they were forced to remain until the day when Warsaw fell. Now Warsaw, beautiful and proud, Warsaw the brilliant lay in ruins. Professor Morris, sitting humped over on the rude bench, thought of the wonderful chance that had brought him were history, tragic and important, was being made. He did not worry greatly over the disappearance of Elinor. He remembered several times in Princeton when she had disappeared. Once they found her under a bed. He wondered whether anyone had looked under the beds in the forsaken house. The terrible idea that his baby girl might be actually lost in the terrible disaster of Warsaw's defeat never once occurred to him. He was annoyed a little at the disturbance she had caused, and resolved to speak very severely to her.

He determined also to reprove Warren for his words; but reflecting on the terrors and excitement and peril of the past hours, he decided to treat it as a little boyish impatience, and overlook the whole thing.

As for his going back to find Elinor, he supposed it would really be a waste of time. Warren would be perfectly able to find her; so he pushed the bench against the wall, snapped a pad from his pocket, was soon lost in pages and pages of notes on the events of the week.

But down in the clothes room while Ivan hastily took off his rich garments and fitted himself with rough work clothes from the shelves, Warren Morris walked the floor and groaned.

"Don't' take it like that, Warren," said Ivan, pausing to place a sympathetic hand on his friend's shoulder.

"It is awful!" groaned Warren. "She is so little, and so easily frightened. I believe it will kill her."

"No, it won't," said Ivan. "There is no coward's blood in Elinor. Wherever she is, she will know we will find her sooner or later. She will be looking out for us every minute. And no one will hurt her. You know people don't take the trouble to drag children off just to kill them. If the three I saw took those girls, they will be careful enough of them, you may be sure. I would rather have them there than with soldiers. The only thing I am hoping is that we can trace them before they leave the city. But I don't believe anyone, even with the best credentials, can get away for the next few days."

"If we had anything for a clue," said Warren. "Can't you even remember what they looked like?"

"Not particularly," said Ivan regretfully. "I would know them if I should see them again. One of the men had a very peculiar walk, but I couldn't describe it to you. It wasn't a limp; just a queer way of using his feet. I don't know whether I would know the woman or not. She looked like hundreds of the sort I have seen down in the open markets, some of them looking a little more so and some less."

"How more so?" asked Warren.

"Why, perhaps fatter, or thinner, or dirtier, but all lawless and no account. I tell you, Warren," he said earnestly, "when I get to be a man, if our house is still in power then, I shall spend my time cleaning up the streets and people of Warsaw. Those old holes and rookeries down by the river, and the streets leading to the wharves have got to be cleaned out or wiped out."

"Better not let my father hear you," said Warren. "He would tell you that all that section is historic, and therefore valuable."

"Perhaps it has been," said Ivan. "But we can always refer to your father's great book on Warsaw, and what the world needs now is light and space and air."

"Well," sighed Warren, "perhaps the book will help some college grind, but if he had let the old thing slide, he would never have lost my sister."

"I do think that we ought to look at it a little from your father's standpoint," said Ivan gently. "You know the children were in the house and the door shut. They were playing contentedly, and he thought it would only take a minute to go upstairs and get the parcel. No doubt he was a good deal longer than he thought he would be, but he thought everything was as safe as it could be. I think we would have done the same thing. Be fair, Warren. Don't you think so?"

"I suppose so," said Warren. "Only now it seems as though it was not safe to leave them a second."

"That's how it has come out," said Ivan, buttoning his blouse, "but that's just the sort of thing no one could foresee. One thing seems certain, if we find them near, or in the house, well and good. If they are not around there somewhere, I believe Evelyn has solved the thing. It doesn't seem possible, though, that anyone could have opened the door, and walked in, and dragged the children right in the house, without the least sound of disturbance reaching your father upstairs. Myself, I don't believe the door was close latched, and it may be the children went out themselves. If they did we will find them soon."

"Elinor has been told a million times never to leave the house," said Warren hopefully.

"And you know she minds," said Ivan. "I think we will find them all right, and Evelyn just imagines things. The woman probably meant just what she said. She doubtless had candles from some church, and clothes and food in the bags. She had enough to last some time, judging from the size and weight."

"I hope so, anyway," said Warren. "Are you nearly ready? If we could only run for it!"

"We can't," said Ivan. "The moment they see you run, you are in danger of being shot down. It won't take long, even if we do have to go slowly."

"Well, let's make a start, if you are ready," said Warren restlessly.

They opened the door and found Evelyn waiting for them. She looked pale and weak, but greeted them quietly.

"Don't be any longer than you can, will you, boys?" she begged. "If she is hurt one of you stay with her, and the other come for me. Don't try to bring her here."

"They won't be hurt," said Warren courageously. "But we won't bring them here at all. We will stay with them, one of us, and come back to tell you. You know they will be together."

"How wicked I am!" said Evelyn. "I forgot little Rika. She has been with us so short a time. I am so thankful she is with Elinor. They will not be so badly frightened."

"Of course not," said Warren. "You go to father, Evvy. We will come soon."

CHAPTER III

IN WARSAW'S BY-WAYS

On the day of Warsaw's downfall, a little girl, perhaps three years of age, wandered to the door of the comfortable old house where the Morrises lived. She was dressed with the greatest richness. She was unable to tell her name, or indeed give the slightest clue to her home or family. Ivan and the servants declared her a child of the nobility, but were unable to gain any information from her broken baby talk. She played contentedly with Elinor all day, and at night when she was prepared for bed, they found secreted under her dress jewels fit for a king. Chains of diamonds and rubies encircled her baby neck, and rings of the greatest value were sewed to her garments, while great brooches were pinned in rows on her little skirts. Professor Morris, after pronouncing the collection worth a couple of hundred thousand dollars, stuffed the lot in a couple of his coat pockets with the remark that he had better put them away!

Evelyn, however, took the jewels, and sewing them securely in a belt, fastened it around her own waist for safekeeping. No one doubted that the pretty child would soon be claimed. They soon discovered that her name was Rika, but more than that she could not tell them. She did not seem to feel very lonely or frightened, although she fretted at bed time, calling over and over some name they could not catch.

Elinor was as delighted with her as though she had been given a beautiful new doll; and now Evelyn felt sure that they would remain together unless parted by force - or death. The last thought struck to her heart like a chill, but she would not admit even the possibility of such a thing. The certainty that the children had been drugged and carried off in the two sacks battled constantly with the hope that the boys would find them playing around the corner, or hidden in some unfrequented spot. So it was with a cheerful trust that she said good-bye to the two young workingmen who presently issued from the door of the great store building, and went rapidly up the desert and torn up street.

They did not dare run. Rather, they slunk along from building to building as though fearful of being seen. When they passed a wrecked chimney, fallen across the street, Warren rubbed some of the soot and grime on his face and clothes, and told Ivan to do the same. He thought very wisely that they looked too clean and neat for the parts they were endeavoring to enact. In addition to the soot, they were soon soiled and torn from scrambling over wreckage and even Evelyn would not have recognized them.

Soon reaching the residence portion of the city, they began an immediate search for Boy Scouts. Out of the hundred or so in their section, they were fortunate enough to find ten. Several of these were searching frantically for relatives and friends. Not one but had lost someone dear to him. They scattered with a will when Warren and Ivan told them about the two children, but the boys who had been nearest the Professor's house, all said that they had not seen the little girls at all. There were no troops moving about that part while the boys were talking and planning, and they were not molested in any way when they scattered and began to search every foot of the neighborhood. Noon found Warren, Ivan, Jack and a couple of others near a wrecked and deserted bakeshop. There was no one to ask and none to object when they scrambled over the heaps of stone and plaster and wood, and tried the doors of the great ovens. Sure enough, there they found, well cooked and safe, a supply of bread and meant and sweets. Warren and Jack were broken-hearted at the absence of the slightest clue to Elinor, but they made a manly effort and managed to eat a good and nourishing meal, because they knew that they must keep up every bit of strength they had.

At three o'clock by agreement they all met at the Professor's house. Not one had secured a single clue. They had searched every empty and ruined building and had asked every person that they had seen. No one had been able to tell them anything that sounded at all helpful. Warren had thought that the fact that the strange child wore a scarlet dress would be the means of tracing them immediately; but according to the people they questioned, half the children in Warsaw had worn scarlet dresses or coats. Warren was sick with despair. After a short talk, the boys scattered again, working out from the Professor's house like the spokes of a wheel for about half a mile. As Warren decided that he had about reached the limit agreed upon, he stood thinking, when the shrill Scout whistle sounded at his right. It was the signal to gather, and Warren's heart leaped with delight as he thought, "Elinor is found."

He crossed the space like a whirlwind, leaping over fallen walls and dashing around buildings in his mad race.

He found the Scout who had whistled standing at the sagging door of what had once been a comfortable home.

"Where is she?" cried Warren as he reached the doorway.

The boy shook his head. He was deathly pale, and trembled.

"It is not your sister; you may be glad of that; but we must do something. Go in!"

Four other Scouts came panting up, all flushed with the hope that Elinor had been found. They followed the boy who had pushed Warren through the hall and through another door. Warren stopped appalled.

Half the wall was gone. A bomb had evidently struck the house. On the bed a young woman lay. She was quite dead. Her ashy face told it without the evidence of the blood in which she was bathed. By her side lay a tiny girl. She, too, was still and cold in the last sleep of death, but by a strange mischance of war, a baby lay unharmed in the young mother's arms.

Unattended, uncomforted and cold, it had lain there for hours; yet it lived, and as the boys entered sent up a feeble wail. Shaken to the heart, Warren walked to the bed and picked up the infant. Its cries had dwindled to a feeble whining, and it shivered. Warren hastily unfastened his blouse, and pressed the little being to the warmth of his body. He could feel it press against him, or so it seemed to him, as he stood there in that chamber of death. His course, however, seemed clear. The living child in his arms must be cared for, and at once. He could only think of Evelyn. The hospitals were either shattered or filled with too many wounded soldiers. There was no room in any place of that sort now for a little baby . Life was cheap in Warsaw that day. He would take it to Evelyn and she would take care of it somehow. His own little Elinor he dared not think of.

It was with an almost breaking heart that he and the other boys rapidly retraced their steps and finally gained the warehouse. As he went up the long stairs, Professor Morris left his corner, and stood ready to greet them. He was smiling.

"Well, well, where is Elinor?" be asked testily.

"We did not find her," answered Warren curtly. He was so tired that he staggered as be walked. He gained the top of the steps and, crossing unsteadily to Evelyn, laid the baby in her arms. Its little pinched face, and bloodstained dress prepared her for Warren's story.

"It is nearly starved," she said. "What shall we give it?"

"I know," said Ivan. "Babies all drink milk, don't they? There is a court down below, and when we went out I saw a couple of goats in it."

It was true, and the poor creatures were glad enough to be milked. The baby, finally fed and warmed, slept exhausted in Evelyn's arms.

In all the cruel war whose dark shadow obscured Europe a great deal of suffering fell to the share of the poor little babies and the small children. To older children war could be explained. It was a vast and terrible something that swept away homes and food and comfort. It was a monster that devoured fathers and brothers, and left families without support, and homeless. But there was a reason that could be told, and which they could understand more or less.

But the tiny ones, alas! What could be told them when their little world tumbled, when they were carried out from warmth and safety, when food was denied; when the bosoms that had warmed them grew cold and unresponsive, what could they do but suffer and die the slow, torturing death of hunger and cold?

Their little cries arose to heaven, there were no ears to hear them when the thunder of guns drowned all else. Poor, poor babies! Born, many of them, to enlighten the world with new discoveries, to cure the afflicted, to bring joy, they have perished as surely or a cause which they could not understand as have the soldiers in the trenches.

When great nations are falling, and men are being mowed down like grass, in numbers beyond the counting, the lives of little babies can only be held precious by mothers who guard them with their every breath.

The poor little bit of humanity found by the boys would soon have closed its little eyes in the death which bad so suddenly overtaken the mother and sister. But it proved a sturdy little scrap, and after drinking all the milk they dared give it, cried for more.

It was a pretty child, well dressed and well cared for, and Evelyn studied it with tender interest as it lay contentedly in her arms. As she hushed and soothed it into sleep, she talked with her brothers. Professor Morris had gone to the other end of the long room, and they could hear him groan as he walked the floor.

"Don't you think that it would be safe now for us to go back home?" said Evelyn. "We can always prove that we are Americans, and I think there will be no more lawlessness. What do you think?"

Warren remembered the soldier with the wounded shoulder.

"We can't leave Peter here," he said.

"Why no, but he managed to get up here with help, and I think we can get him home with us. I don't know what else to do, unless Anna is willing to stay with him until morning."

"That's the thing to do," said Warren, "but Anna is such a scare cat."

"She ought to be willing to stay with her own brother!" declared Evelyn. "That shoulder will kill him unless cold water is kept on it all the time, until we can get hold of a doctor or get him to a hospital."

"The hospitals are so full that you can't get inside the doors," said Warren.

"I found that out today."

"Well, we will ask Anna, anyway," she said. She called to the governess, who approached at once. Telling her the plan, Evelyn waited for the woman to speak.

"Surely that is a wise plan indeed," she said, to their great relief. "Peter could not be moved tonight. He is full of fever. And someone will find our little Elinor, and take her home. Then what could they do if the house was deserted?"

"I never thought of that," said Evelyn in a grief-stricken tone. "Let us hurry and get back before it is dark."

"Yes," said Warren, "we could not make it at all in the dark. The lights are all gone, and the streets are nearly impassable in lots of places. Get dad, and come on. Don't forget the book," he added, smiling bitterly.

They hastily brought blouses and overalls from the clothes room below and made as comfortable a bed for Peter as they could. There was plenty of goat's milk to drink, and bread from the bake shop, with which Warren had thoughtfully had the boys fill their pockets.

Then, as the dusk gathered, they hurried out, Professor Morris clasping the bulky manuscript, Evelyn carrying the sleeping baby, while Warren and Ivan supported her on either side, and Jack went ahead to pick out the safest path.

They reached the house after a hard walk, and were soon feeling some sense of bodily comfort after all the hardships of the day. They decided to act as nearly as possible as though they were but little disturbed by the past events, and to assume the position of foreigners who felt themselves under the protection of their own government.

Naturally, all their thoughts were of Elinor, but night had fallen black and stormy, and in all the confusion and lawlessness there was nothing to be done but wait as best they could for morning.

In spite of his anxiety, Warren slept heavily and did not awaken until his sister shook him, and he opened his eyes to find that it was seven, 7 o'clock.

"No news, Warren dear," said Evelyn. "Only that that poor little baby is certainly better. Oh, Warren, it is so cunning! I do hope it will be all right. I want to keep it if we do not find its father. All the rest of its family must be dead." She sat down on the edge of Warren's bed. "Do you know," she said, "I feel as though everyone besides ourselves is hurt or lost or dead or kidnapped? I have been thinking what I would do if anyone kidnapped me. I would try so hard to leave some sort of a message. I think if I had my diamond ring on, I would try to scratch something on a window pane."

Warren smiled. "Try some other plan, Evvy," he said. "They wouldn't be apt to wait while you found a window and scratched a letter on it."

"You never can tell," said the girl. "Anyhow, that is what I would try to do. Get up now, Warren, I have a nice hot breakfast for you. Ivan is dressed and has been out getting things to eat."

Warren hurried down and enjoyed the nice breakfast his sister had prepared. Jack, who had had his meal earlier, was awkwardly holding the baby, and seemed quite overcome by the task.

Breakfast over, Warren went with Ivan to the door, and stood for a moment looking down the street. A couple of men, very evil looking and dark browed, approached slowly, and passed on in the direction of the open market. Ivan glanced carelessly at the pair, then stifled an exclamation of surprise. As they reached a safe distance, lie clutched Warren by the arm.

"Look, look!" he cried. "Those are the two men who were with the woman with the sacks."

"What!" cried Warren tensely. "Come!" He started out, and together they followed the two men.

"What are you going to do?" asked Ivan.

"Shadow them until I find where they stay. That woman is no doubt there, wherever that is."

"I follow," said Ivan briefly.

Warren paused. "You can't come," he said regretfully. "Someone has got to look after dad, and as this is a dangerous job, it is my right, as the older, to do it. I wish you could come, but you see how it is, don't you?"

"I suppose so," said Ivan mournfully, "but get back so soon as you can. And if you find Elinor, and need help about getting her away, come back or send, and I will bring all the Scouts down."

The boys shook hands and parted, Ivan hurrying back to the house with the news, while the soiled work boy slouched along after the two skulking villains ahead.

At the open market a few hucksters, braver than most, were selling meat and vegetables to as many as dared come and buy. The men ahead bought freely as though money was plenty. Laden down with supplies, they finally turned and, walking rapidly, plunged down toward the river where the narrow, twisted streets invited criminals of every kind.

Warren, following them as far off as possible, had to act and think quickly at times in order to keep track of them. Finally they turned into a street or alley leading directly to the river, and as Warren hurried after them they disappeared as suddenly as though they had sunk into the earth. Warren darted forward.

It was a row of dismal, crowded houses, and Warren was too far away to know just where the men had turned in. They had disappeared within one of the doors, and Warren walked openly and boldly along, studying each house. It was a rash and reckless thing to do.

Warren forgot the teachings of his order, for there is nothing more persistently urged on a Boy Scout than caution. If Warren had not been so intensely excited, he would have remembered this. But of course his excitement was an excuse for forgetting. It is when we are in dangerous and exciting situations that we must train ourselves to have every faculty at our command.

It is the commonest thing in the world to hear people tell what they might have done, and unfold plans conceived after the necessity for them was past. Such plans make good reading, but poor history.

Warren, of course, tramping hastily down a deserted street, lay open to disaster, and the defeat of his purpose. If he had reconnoitered as carefully as he had followed his game, he would have been able to locate them without the least suspicion on their part that they had been shadowed. It then would have been simple to have watched for some unguarded moment, when the boys could easily have gained entrance to their quarters and secured the children.

There is no great deed accomplished in this world where caution does not play a great part. In war, in business, in sports, the man who looms the biggest after the game is done and people have the time to study things, is the man who had never once failed to exercise a proper amount of caution. In a fairy story this warning is given: "Be bold; be bold - but not too bold."

You see caution does not question or hesitate or delay too long. Caution keeps right on, but slowly and with a careful regard to safe footing. Caution keeps you from rocking the boat, and pointing the loaded gun, and skating near the thin ice. It keeps you from the heels of the kicking horse. It makes the good general save his men.

Warren forgot. After blocks and blocks of trailing, he bolted down the street, examining each house with

George Durston

anxious excitement.

Finally he discovered footmarks leading toward a dark, heavy door, and he stood looking the place over. It was a tall, narrow place which had, centuries past, been used as a dwelling. What it was at present Warren could not guess, unless it had fallen to the level of the damp, rat infested hovel where crime and disease are bred daily in old towns like Warsaw. Strange carvings of dragons and monsters upheld the eaves and formed the heavy water spouts. The tiny, windows were bare and curtainless. They swung open in the wind that blew from the Vistula.

Warren stood looking. He was all alone in the street

CHAPTER IV

HOT ON THE TRAIL

The men had disappeared, and there seemed no further need for caution. As Warren approached nearer, he noted the dark, tumbledown building, which looked as though it had been a ruin for centuries, dismal and uninhabited. Only one thing was noteworthy. The door, a stout one heavily barred with ornamental straps of ancient and rusty iron, was fitted with strong, modern hinges, and had been closely fitted in anew frame. Warren's keen eye quickly grasped these details as he sauntered past, and stopped before 'the building, but what he did not see, and could not guess, was the tiny auger hole bored close to one of the iron frets. Behind that hole stood a man in whose cunning brain suspicion lurked; and Warren did not know that after that close scrutiny the trained eye of one of the basest murderers and criminals in Poland would now recognize him, no matter where they met.

Warren knew that he must gain access to the den, but how?

Thinking rapidly, he resolved to wait until the men again left the place, when he would rap at the door, and try to get in on whatever excuse he might need to invent when the moment arrived. He crossed the street, and entered an abandoned building. For two hours he waited in. biding, never suspecting the anxious scrutiny he himself was undergoing.

His wrist watch told him that noon was past. There was no

George Durston

sign of life in the street. Remembering the loads of provisions that the men had carried, he decided that they did not intend to come out of their hiding place until nightfall. That would give him time to return, report to the anxious watchers at home, and consult with Ivan and the other Boy Scouts.

With Warren, to decide was to act. He hurried through the shattered streets, wondering what the careful Evelyn had kept for him to eat.

As he turned the corner he saw before the house a group of people who seemed to be regarding it curiously. Warren hastened his steps. Pushing through the group, he entered. The door, torn from its hinges, swung against the wall. In the hall a heavy chest of drawers was overturned and the drawers piled together on the floor. The contents were scattered everywhere. Calling the names of the family, Warren dashed through the rooms, vainly hoping to find some trace of his people, or some explanation of the new disaster. Returning to the door, he appealed to the bystanders. What had happened? They told him that they had come down the street just in time to see the soldiers leading off a group of people. More than that they did not know. They supposed that they were now dead. It was what happened in war.

Warren returned to the house, his head whirling. This seemed the last and most crushing blow. To have such a thing happen just as he was about to rescue his little sister and reunite the family! He could not imagine why this thing should have been done. Why should any soldiers molest American citizens?

Utterly overcome, he sank down in a chair by the window and leaned his head on the sill. All gone! He did not know what to do. His quick and clever brain for the moment refused to act. He raised his head and looked dully out into the street where the group of curious people was slowly moving away. For a long time he stared, then his eyes suddenly set themselves on something nearer. Dumfounded, unbelieving, he glared. It seemed that he could hear Evelyn's voice, Evelyn's own words.

"If anyone kidnapped me," she had said, "I think if I had my diamond on I would try to scratch a message on the window pane."

Indeed, her mother's ring had served her well. Before Warren's eyes, on the glass, Evelyn had left her message:

"Arrested as spies. Ac't dad's book. Taken to camp. Find Ivan. Tell Consul. Help."

Clutching the arms of his chair, Warren sat staring at the message on the window pane. He read it over and over. A curious feeling that his eyes were tricking him possessed him. He reached out and rubbed the message slowly, fully expecting it to disappear. The letters felt rough under his fingers. It was really written there with Evelyn's diamond. Still unbelief possessed him. How had it happened that she had foreseen this dreadful mischance clearly enough, in some mysterious way, to plan the delivery of the saving message?

As Warren looked, the events of the last few crowded days seemed to rise up and bear him down under their horror and immensity. He sat clutching the arms of his chair, and with unseeing eyes stared and stared at the letters. All at once he felt very young, very helpless, very lonely.

America, his own dear country, with its safety and its careless, unthinking haphazard hospitality for every living person who seeks her shores; America seemed suddenly to be set farther than the farthest star.

Like most American boys, Warren was clever, shrewd and ingenious. Life with Professor Morris had trained him in ingenuity and efficiency. Since his earliest remembrance it had fallen to his lot to act as the head of his family, making decisions that usually are the sole right of fathers and guardians. But now, under conditions of horror and tragedy, he realized that he was after all only a boy; and the thought came to him that he and his, dear and infinitely precious as they were to each other, counted not at all in the great tragedy of war.

Who was there to help? The American Consul was powerless for the time, if he could be found. Warren knew that the portion of the city where he had lived was a shapeless ruin.

The boy continued to sit motionless in his chair, desperately, desperately puzzling the dark mystery.

Gradually in Warren's dazed mind the whole affair took definite shape. They were gone; arrested on suspicion. For the moment at least he felt sure they were safe, even in the hands of an enemy who had shown themselves utterly cruel and heartless. He felt sure that if they were suspected of being spies every effort would be made to make them confess before they were executed, if it did indeed come near that question.

But "Find Ivan." What did that mean? Evidently Ivan was not with them. As though in answer to his thought, Warren heard or thought he heard a faint shout. He listened. It was repeated, with a sound of pounding and banging. Once more Warren searched the house, beginning with the old dusty, rambling attic set close under the great beams of the old house. Down he hurried, from room to room, looking in presses, under beds, and listening in each room.

As he reached the kitchen, the sound seemed clearer. It was Ivan's voice. He opened the cellar stairs and went down. Once, years, even generations past, the house had been the residence of a noble. The cellar was not the one or two rooms of the modern house. It was vast and vaulted and contained a dozen dark, unlighted apartments, all with heavy, iron-barred, oaken doors.

Professor Morris said that two of the rooms had been used as dungeons and it was in one of these that Warren found Ivan. He stumbled over him as be opened the door. The boy was bound, but lying on his back, so had been able to hammer on the door with his feet. The sound of pounding had carried even better than his shouts.

Warren hastily untied the cords that secured him and helped him up the stairs. He was stiff and sore from the cramped position, but once in the upper rooms, he took a deep breath, and proceeded to tell Warren the events of the morning.

Once more Professor Morris was the cause of the disaster. The Professor was, fortunately, of uncommon type. He was a modest man - so modest that it even ceased to be a virtue, and became an annoying and irritating trait. He never stood up for himself, nor for his family in any way.

The saying, "Generous to a fault" likewise applied to him. He was a spendthrift in kindness, giving not only money needed for himself and the children, but bestowing his time when he needed it himself. His learning he gave recklessly, too, writing long, learned articles for little or no pay, and without a thought that the material given away was just so much capital.

But of one thing he was jealous, careful and touchy. His book, his almost completed work on Warsaw. It was to be a book of books, so clear, so accurate, so full of new f acts that it would be a treasure among the literary treasures of his time. Professor Morris believed in the book with the conviction that comes to writers when they have done something really good. He knew it was fine. It was more than a history of the beautiful and fated city. It was written in such golden, flowing English that the hardest and driest facts in its pages were polished and placed like jewels of great price in their descriptive setting. And they were jewels. He had mined them out of strange places in that ancient town. He had taken his time and in digging for his beloved facts, he had found many an unexpected wonder.

Knowing his father as he did, Warren could see the story told by Ivan as plainly as though he had been present. One thing made him smile as he recalled it. His father would not use a typewriter, and anything written in his strange, cramped hand would look suspicions at once. And he knew, too, that his father would resent even the touch of strangers on the beloved pages. He smiled a little bitterly.

"Go on, Ivan," he said. "Let's hear it all."

"A detachment of soldiers came down the street," said Ivan, rubbing his lame muscles, "and as they came they looked through every house. I suppose they were on the lookout for troops of our soldiers. When they reached this place, your father met them at door and talked a moment with the officer in charge. Of course Evelyn and I did not know what they said, but the officer grew angry and your father just stood there and smiled and shook his head. Then Evelyn went to your father and as soon as the officer saw her he bowed very low, and in English said, 'Prettee, prettee.' Evelyn came back to us and took the baby from Jack.

"Then the door slammed, and we heard the big bolt fall, and your father dragged that big chest across it and came in as pleased as could be. He said, 'There, I have settled that! Such impertinence! They wanted to search my house!'

"But at that, blows fell on the door and presently it fell and the soldiers rushed in. Your father had his book and was trying to hide it in the lining of a chair. Of course they at once thought it must be plans or something of the sort, and Professor would not tell them a thing and we couldn't because we could not make them understand that it was just a book about the history of Warsaw.

When they took it from your father, of course he resisted, and that settled the matter. We had to go to the headquarters. Of course, your father would have followed his book wherever that went. As we started, the officer took Evelyn by the arm, and I think I hit him pretty hard for it. Anyway he gave a command, and a dozen big fellows took me and tied me up and carried me down here. It is a good thing you came, Warren." He shuddered as he thought of the possible ending that his adventure might have had.

Warren was deep in thought. One event pressed so closely on another that things lost their significance and importance.

"We have got to get a hustle on now," he said.

"Your American hustle-on; that means act quickly, does it not?" said Ivan. "We must indeed hustle on. Let us find where they are, and then apply to your Consul."

"That's all right," said Warren, "but I don't think they are in any immediate danger and I think the first thing to do is to got hold of Elinor."

"Get hold of her," said Ivan. "Do you know where she is?"

"Yes, I think I have found her," said Warren and commencing at the moment when the boys parted on the street, be gave Ivan an account of his morning's discoveries.

"Good! Good!" said Ivan. "We will go together this time, and together we will rescue our pretty little Elinor. Have you made any plans?"

"No, I haven't," confessed Warren. "I don't know what ails me; I seem to be perfectly brainless today. It looks like I am losing everybody that belongs to me."

Ivan shrugged his shoulders. "Look at me," he said. "My mother long dead, my father somewhere on the field of battle, or lying dead in the trenches. I do not know; but I must not think. What I want to do is to save Professor Morris, my second father, and Evelyn and Jack and Elinor, who are as sisters and brother to me. Let us start and plan as we go."

"Have you any money?" asked Warren. "I have not a single copper."

"Nor I, " said Ivan.

"We ought to have some," said Warren. "We might have to bribe those people."

Ivan laughed, and felt down his blouse. "This might help," he said. "I hate to give the small one up. It has been in the family, always worn by the eldest son, for more generations than I know; but if we have to give it, it will come back. It always has." He offered Warren two rings, magnificent jewels.

Warren shook his head. "I hope we won't have to use them," he said.

"What of that?" said Ivan. "Jewels, even family jewels, do not count for much beside the dear ones. Ah, Warren," said Ivan, "it is hard for boys to talk, even here in Poland, where it is easier to say what is in one's heart than it seems to be with you Americans. But let me tell you now all that I think. We do not know what we may get into today, what peril - maybe death. I feel danger approaching; I cannot say how. All the people of my house have been able to foresee disaster. What it is I know not. So I will say that so long as I do live, I will never cease to love you and yours. I want you to take this ring that we have held so long and if we are parted, wear it for the sake of Prince Ivan of Poland."

Warren swallowed hastily. "Same here!" he said. "You know darned well I'm strong for you, Old Ivy Scout." He felt hastily in all his pockets. "Haven't a thing to swap," be continued, "not a - " He drew out his hand with something in it. "Guess this will have to do," he said. "It's a buffalo nickel, but I brought it from home. You can have it."

"Thank you so much. I will always keep it," said Ivan. It was so. Years after, if Warren could have looked into the future, he would have seen a magnificent figure at court, one decoration on his jeweled breast being a coin around which sparkled a double row of priceless diamonds. The coin was only, a nickel but that mattered not to Prince Ivan.

As the boys approached the street where Warren had located the house of the thieves, they decided to hide for a little in the ruins across the street, and watch for awhile in the hope that the door might open, or the two men come out.

They made the approach one at a time, and settled down for a long wait. An hour or more went by, and all at once Warren stuck out a long leg and noiselessly kicked Ivan. The oaken door across the street was ajar. Just a crack, and for a long time it remained so, while the boys scarcely breathed.

It opened slowly, and the two men came cautiously out. They did not glance across the street, but looking carefully up and down the crooked alley, closed the door carelessly, and went off at a brisk gait without a glance behind.

The boys looked at each other.

"Now!" said Ivan.

"Wait!" answered Warren. "Give them time. No doubt they will be gone most of the night."

There was a long silence, then glancing at his watch, Warren said, "Come! Do you see that door? They did not latch it. I don't believe there is a soul over there but the woman. There is just one thing to do. Go over and look in; and if she is alone we will rush her, tie her up and get off with the children. We can do it."

"That's the only thing to do," said Ivan. "Let's go."

The street was deserted as they crossed it and stepped close to the oaken door. It was ajar, and they could see the interior of the dark, prison-like room. The woman was there bending over a pot that swung on a crane in the fireplace. A heap of filthy rags was in a corner near by, and lying there was little

George Durston

Elinor and the strange child Rika. A sob rose in Warren's throat as he saw his sister, so pale and thin and terrified she looked. He heard Ivan's breath come sharply.

"Let's rush!" he said.

"You can't!" answered Ivan. "Don't you see the chain on the inside of the door?"

"It's light, we can break that," answered Warren. "Get yourself together. When I say three, throw your whole weight. Grab the woman as quickly as you can."

"All right," said Ivan.

Warren stepped back a space and held himself for a spring.

"One, two," he counted slowly. "Three" was never uttered. He heard a strange cry from Ivan; and as he did so, a frightful blow from some heavy, blunt instrument struck him squarely. He crumpled down unconscious.

Ivan, behind him, evaded the blow aimed at his head by the second ruffian, and quick as a panther stood back to the wall, gazing at his assailant.

"Hands down," said the man, grinning evilly. "Hands down before I brain you!"

"What do you want with us?" demanded Ivan.

The man laughed.

"What would we want of eavesdroppers and spies? This is our house, poor as it is. We will guard it when young thieves like you come peering in the cracks.

What did you think to steal of honest men as poor as yourselves? Your friend here deserves his broken head. Must I give you one, or will you come with me peaceably?"

"I'll come if you will tell me what you are going to do with us," said Ivan.

Again the man laughed, and with his foot shoved the body of Warren lying motionless on the ground.

"Come on," said the other man. "Why waste words? Get hold of him and bring him along!"

"Let me have my way," said the man standing over Ivan. "This amuses me. Come, come, young one, what will you - obedience or a broken head?"

Ivan was silent, then he spoke. "I won't fight," he said. "You are too big, but I won't go in that door with you."

"So!" said the man. "Then we do it in this fashion." He made a rush at Ivan and seizing him in his arms, held him until the other man lifted Warren and so, half carrying and half dragging Ivan, he followed through the dungeon-like doorway into the gloom and chill of the great room beyond.

CHAPTER V

IN THE ENEMY'S HANDS

Ivan's first impression was of a dead, heavy chill which the fire burning in the great fireplace at the other end of the vast room was powerless to lighten. The place was half underground, and what light entered was filtered through dusty and cobwebbed panes of leaded glass set high under the vaulted roof. The windows partially lighted the heavy oak beams which supported the ceiling, but the lower parts of the room lay in deep shadow. Emblems and rude pictures were scratched and chalked on the walls, but Ivan could not make them out in the dim light.

Running the width of the room before the fireplace was a massive table, and on either side of it were benches built where they stood. From the size and strength of them, they might have been intended for the use of a race of giants or exceedingly fat men! Their carved bases spread heavily apart, and huge dragon claw feet braced them on the floor which, beneath and around the table, was carefully paved with stone.

At one side of the fireplace a great pile of wood was placed, broken and splintered pieces picked up from the buildings which had been shelled by the great guns of the enemy. Bits of oaken beams, pieces of rare, highly polished furniture, and scraps of priceless carvings made the pile which soon would go in flames to cook the wretched supper even then in course of preparation.

A woman stood by the table, scraping scales from a fish. A heavy knife was in her hand, and as she raised her dark and scowling face Ivan recognized her and shuddered.

As she stood watching the entrance of the group at the door, scowling and peering through the gloom, she looked to Ivan's eyes like one of the furies of the French Revolution. All the history he had read of that dreadful period was made clear and real to him. Ivan, closely watched, and closely guarded from harm, had up to the time of the bombardment of Warsaw, never come in contact with anyone out of his own noble class with the exception of the Morris family. His father, knowing the educational standing of Professor Morris in America, and judging the whole family by his mild, inoffensive manner, had decided to allow Ivan, his son, to learn English from The Professor. It had not occurred to him, a man of many affairs, to suspect the presence of an ingenious lively, mischievous whirlwind in the person of the Professor's elder son.

When Ivan told his father with enthusiasm of the Professor's family, the Prince imagined them of course to be exactly like the Professor, and rejoiced that Ivan could be among such studious and book loving, quiet people. So he told Ivan that he might spend what time he liked with the Morris family, and then forgot the whole thing in the fearful question of War which soon arose. When he left for the Russian front he left orders that in case of any peril or disaster Ivan was to go to the Morris house and there remain for greater safety.

Before the happenings of the last chapter, however, Ivan had been almost constantly with Warren for a year, and had so imbibed his democratic ideas and had studied so hard to make good as a Scout that Prince Ivan the Magnificent, had he returned, would have had difficulty in recognizing his only and dearly loved son.

But as a matter of fact, Ivan the Magnificent did not return. Instead, blood stained, mud stained and distorted, he slept in a far away trench past which had swept the invaders' line, grim and terrible.

He had fought well and desperately for the honor of Poland until at last, under a leaden rain, Ivan the Prince had gone to meet the fate of Ivan the Man. And not one word of this did Ivan the boy suspect.

It had never seemed that harm could touch his wonderful father. He must be safe; and Ivan moved through his many adventurous days with only the thought that he would have so much more to tell his father on one of the rare and precious evenings when Prince Ivan's duties at court and with his regiment would allow him to spend a few happy hours with his son.

So it was with a keen and appraising eye that Ivan viewed that dark and dungeon- like interior, thinking to tell his father all about it.

The woman beside the table scowled darkly as she saw the group.

"What now?" she demanded. "Are those the spies? They are nothing but boys! Why do you bother with them, Michael Paovla, why did you bring them here? Crack them on the head! The river runs swift enough down the street there."

She brandished her knife as she spoke.

"I will not give them one single meal, do, you hear that?"

"Peace, Martha! Do not jest," said the large man with a wry smile.

He looked at Ivan as he spoke.

"Who are you?" he asked. Clothed as the boy was in mean and soiled garments, there was still something distinguished about him.

He stood proudly erect. Perhaps his name would help out.

"Ivan Ivanovich, of the House of Sabriski," he said, looking the man in the face.

The three shouted with laughter. "Isn't he clever?" cried the woman. "Ask him something else!"

"No," said the man. "I want to think that over. Come, it is cold here!"

He picked Warren up from the floor where he had thrown him, and, carrying him down the long room, made his way around the great table and dropped him roughly on the pile of rags where, Elinor and Rika were crouched.

Poor little Elinor, huddled on her pile of rags, did not recognize the limp burden carried in by the larger of the two men, whom she had learned to dread with unspeakable terror. When he threw it down in the middle of the room, the pale face was turned toward the child, and she recognized, Warren. She commenced to scream. Shriek after shriek left her pale lips, and the man started over to her side, when a short, sharp word silenced her. She looked to see who had spoken, calling her so familiarly by name.

"Stop, Elly, stop," said the voice in English, and her cries were stilled as by magic, although she still gazed with longing and terror at the pale face down which a tiny line of blood trickled.

The second man clasped a second boy, dirty and torn, and meanly dressed in a workman's blouse. She stared at him, never recognizing Ivan, whom she bad always seen so gorgeously clothed in furs and fine broadcloth and exquisite linen. It was not until he spoke again that she recognized him.

"Be quiet, Elinor," he said. "We will save you. Warren is not hurt, he is just dizzy. He will be all right soon."

Ivan spoke hopefully, but as he looked down at the boy lying before him, he wondered in his heart if there was really a spark of life left in that still, pale, bleeding body. As for Elinor, after the first outburst, she sat dumbly trembling.

The past day and night bad been so crowded with horrors that the tender children were fast passing into a state where they neither realized nor felt the hardships and abuse they were subjected to.

The time when they sat playing in Professor Morris's quiet house seemed too far away to remember.

They bad been playing happily, the two children, when the family decided to go away for a few hours, but so happily were they with their dolls and each other, that they paid no attention to the stir and unrest about them. Even Elinor, who was almost six years old, had not concerned herself with the sound of the big guns.

She did not notice when her father left the room. If he told her, as he thought be had, to "sit quietly" and await his return, she failed to hear him. So she took Rika by the hand and. "went, visiting." They sat down on the top step, and looked into the empty street, and watched occasional groups of fleeing Poles hurry past to the safety of the plains. A rough looking woman came past, noticed them, and returned, looking as she did so at the house, and peering into the hall through the open door.

Then she approached the children and in a, voice she tried in vain to make soft, she asked what they were doing, and who they were.

Little Rika, who could say but few words, sat and stared at her with a frown.

Elinor answered politely. The woman studied them carefully. Elinor was a child whose beauty was always remarked wherever she went, and the little Rika was equally lovely. They had been used to kindness and attention from everyone, so when the woman took out a queer little box, and offered them each a funny little black candy, they accepted them quite as a matter of course. Then she drew back, and the children turned to their dolls again. But only for a moment. Then the head of golden curls and the long, black ringlets drooped and the drugged children were asleep. The woman shook two big sacks out from beneath her dress, and as coolly and as cruelly as though she was filling them with straw, she shoved a child in either bag, crossed to the curb with her heavy burden, and sat down to wait.

When her two accomplices joined her, they went rapidly to the hovel where Warren had tracked them hater, and releasing the half smothered and unconscious children, they laid them down on a pile of rags, and sat looking at them, while they ate their evening portion of black bread and cold fish.

There was a great discussion. The larger man, Michael, was in favor of offering the children for a ransom. The others would not consider it at all.

"Remember," said Martha, the woman, "there is much danger in collecting such fees. Rather will I prepare these little ladies for the trade of beggars. So beautiful are they that I can go through every capital in Europe, if so Europe still stands."

"Have it your own way," said the smaller man, Patro by name.

"I always do," she said simply. Then she studied the sleeping forms again.

"I think it will be well, some time soon, to twist the legs of the small one," she said. "She would make a sweet cripple."

"No!" said Michael. "You may not do so. I will not have it."

The woman laughed. "Said I not that I have my own way?" she asked.

"All right, Martha, you do," said Patro, "but believe me, it is better to take the greatest care of those little ones. Think what dancers they may make some day. There is a fortune in those little feet, I'll be bound. Be careful of them, watch them, and perhaps some day they may be prancing on the opera stage at St. Petersburg, or even here in Warsaw."

The woman sat thinking for a little. "Perhaps you are right," she said. "People are dance-mad these times. They are pretty enough to climb to any heights."

Patro laughed.

"Why laugh?" said Martha angrily.

"Nothing, nothing, dear Martha, only that it is funny to think you are taking these children down from the heights where they belong so that they may climb back for your pleasure."

The woman's brow grew black. She reached out a heavy foot, and pushed Elinor away from her.

"Not for thy pleasure," she said sneeringly.

"No, Patro, no! They are to pay me over and over for my life. Drop for drop, pain for pain, I will take from them all I have myself suffered. They shall sleep cold, because so I slept all my childhood. They shall hunger because I did so. They shall beg in the streets while I listen. Ah!" she shook her fists above her head, "I have hated all the world, and now these shall pay me!"

Patro shrugged his shoulders. "As you will," he said. "They are coming to life again, however. I would advise you to feed them enough to keep beauty in their faces and grace in their limbs, if you indeed wish to use them for food and light and fire."

"That is sound sense, Patro," she answered, and when the children came dizzily to consciousness again, she treated them with almost a rough kindness. But when they cried, she beat them, taking pains to let the blows fall where they would not leave visible scars or bruises.

So passed the dragging hours, until Warren, unconscious and bleeding, was flung down at Elinor's side.

"There!" said Michael. "You will spy, will you? Well, we have you now. And when next you walk the streets, if so you do, you will have cause to remember Michael Paovla and his friends."

Patro frowned. "You are too handy with names," he said. "Trust only a dead dog."

"Leave that to me," said Michael with a dark frown. "You," he said to Ivan, "you see this gun? We'll not bind you, but if you stir toward the door, or make a move to free yourself, you are lost. I will shoot you down."

"We only want the children," said Ivan boldly. "Give them to us, and we will go away, and you will not be harmed."

The three set up a shout of laughter. "Thanks, thanks!" said Michael when he could speak, but Martha said angrily, "What! Give up my fire and light and food? Not much!"

"Suppose I pay you," said Ivan, "I will reward you well."

Again a shout went up.

"A million thanks," said the woman. "What will you give - a dozen dried fishes?"

"You don't know me," scowled Ivan proudly. "I am the son of your Prince, Ivan the Brilliant. Beware how you treat me and these friends of mine."

"The boy will kill me!" cried the woman, leaning back and wiping the tears of mirth from her leathery cheeks. "Go on, go on, my prince. And will you not ask us to the palace some day soon? We would like to see you at your own home."

'Give us the children and set us free, and you may come," said Ivan after a pause.

"No; you are too amusing," said the woman. "Rather we will take you with us, or else leave you safely locked here where no one shall disturb you."

Ivan looked at the worn and haggard children and the form of Warren now stirring slightly, then he handed the great ruby to Michael.

"Take, this and let us go," he pleaded.

The man looked wonderingly at the flashing stone. "So you too help yourself in these war times?" he said sneeringly. "What else do you carry, little rat?"

He ran a practiced, light fingered hand over Ivan, searching for more jewels, but of course found none.

Night seemed to come all at once in the dark and partly underground room. Warren, untended, came slowly back to consciousness, and lay where he had fallen in a sort of doze. Little Elinor crept to him and, laying her head on his shoulder, went to sleep. Presently Martha began to yawn, and the men nodded where they sprawled on the benches. The woman drew out an armful of rags, and prepared for the night by wrapping another shawl around her shoulders.

The men rose after a whispered consultation, and taking Ivan to the furthest and darkest corner, tied him securely to a ring in the wall. His bonds were loose enough to permit him to lie down on the hard earth and stone floor, but he sat with his back against the wall, wide awake, every nerve tense and quivering.

Twice Michael came and looked at him in the light of a torch from the fire, and retreated muttering. Ivan decided to pretend sleep. The third time Michael gave a grunt of satisfaction.

He went back to the fire and beckoned the others from their pallets.

"He is dead asleep," he said in a low whisper. "We must make our plans."

"Good!" said the woman. "What do you want to do about it?"

She too whispered in a low tone and it struck Ivan that for some strange reason he was listening to a conversation spoken in tones that ordinarily could not be heard three feet away from the speakers. He listened intently. Every syllable was clear and distinct. Owing to some peculiar formation of the vaulted ceiling, the sounds were brought to him, forty feet from the speakers, as accurately as though spoken into a telephone. Ivan's courage rose once more.

He heard the man Michael light his pipe.

"I don't know," he said.

"Of course not!" sneered the woman. "You never do! I suppose you don't want to kill them?"

"What's the use?" asked the man. "Why blacken our souls further than we must?"

"I'll tell you why," said Martha suddenly. Her whisper cut like a knife. "I'll tell you. Because I fear them. Boys as they are, I fear them! There is a spirit in the eyes of the one who calls himself Ivan that will never die until death blinds them. The little rat! The smart little rat! Calling himself a prince! My, I wish I had had the training of him. Well, whoever he is, he is a

Pole, and he will hurt us yet. I feel it. I can feel it, anyway, that harm will come to us through those boys. I warn you, Michael. Patro, I warn you.

Once, twice, thrice! You know I never fail."

There was a silence, and Ivan heard Patro catch his breath sharply.

"Well, what would you?" he said finally.

There was a note of triumph in the woman's voice when she spoke.

"Tomorrow night," she said, "we will leave them here, tied to the table. I will leave food on the table for them, just enough for one meal. I have still my little friends in the pill box on the chimney ledge. They are as strong as ever. We will not stay to see whether they eat or not. But I think they will, because I will see to it that they do not taste much food tomorrow. We will lock the door. I will go down to Prague. They say it is but little harmed, and I have a sister there. I will give the smaller child to her. I have a fancy for the light one myself, and they are too unlike to pass off for sisters."

There was a long pause. Then, "Have it as you like," said Michael. "Of course, the boys will bother a good deal, if they go free."

"Certainly they would," said Martha. "We would never know where they would crop up, especially that Ivan one."

"Suppose they do not eat?" asked Patro.

"Eat, eat!" cried Martha. "Well, know you nothing of boys! And they will suspect nothing. You are brutes, brutes, remember, and I so kind and so sorry," she laughed. "They will believe all I say," she added.

Michael nodded. "Then it is settled," he said.

In the United States, every possible precaution is taken to protect children from harm. Laws are made especially for their safety; societies exist in every town and city to look after them. They go unharmed through the streets. Noble men and women give their lives to visiting the poorest districts and making easier the lot of the unfortunate ones they find there. Special cases are frequently written up in the papers, and help found for them in that way. In factories, shops, stores, asylums, in the streets, in the slums, every possible, effort is made to make the lot of children an easier and happier one.

In a great number of the European countries, the case is different. There are no laws, for instance, governing the age at which a child shall be put to work. In fact, in order to keep body and soul together, children labor from the time they are babies. They do the work of farm animals when their little hands can scarcely grasp the implements of toil. There are many, oh, so many of them; and they are held cheaply. Poorly clothed, poorly fed, they take kindly to theft, as a means of getting the necessities of their bare, miserable little lives.

Once upon a time, there was a dark and dreadful age when making cripples and dwarfs was a regular trade. Children were taken (nearly always stolen ones) and their limbs twisted, or their faces distorted, in order to gain sympathy from the passersby, of whom they were taught to beg. That frightful time is long past; but the trades of begging and thieving are still taught.

And to criminals like those in whose hands the children had fallen, life, and child life especially, was too cheap and of too little account to matter much. They did not in the least mind the contemplation of a crime as horrible as the one they had just decided on. They were afraid of the bright, alert Scouts who had fallen into their clutches, and to them there was but one way to treat the matter - the shackles and the poisoned food.

CHAPTER VI

TO THE RESCUE

After this there was silence. The men slept with snores and grunts an they moved uneasily on their hard beds, and Ivan slept only at intervals. He was anxious to know whether the conversation had been heard by Warren, but did not dare to communicate with him in any way, although he could hear an occasional sigh as though his friend was suffering pain. Warren was indeed feeling badly from the blow that had nearly broken his skull. Fortunately the weapon, a piece of iron shod wood, had glanced and so saved his life. But his head ached worse than he had thought a head could ache; and when he finally came out of the, daze of the blow, he slept only in a sort of stupor. He had not heard the conversation that had been listened to so eagerly by Ivan, and so was at least saved that anxiety.

Day came, and to Ivan, who was prepared, there were signs of departure. Warren, who still lay silent on his pallet of rags, did not seem to see anything. He did not eat, but accepted a cup of water from the woman's hand.

Elinor clung to him, and the woman did not object.

Ivan was afraid to speak to any of them. The day dragged away, and finally (it seemed years) the room grew so dark that Ivan knew that night must be approaching. Soon he would know their fate. It was uncertain, because he knew that at any time in the day they might have decided not to leave their death to the poisoned food, but to shoot them to death before leaving the place.

However, Martha commenced the preparation of the meal that was meant for supper, and Ivan noticed that she had made more than usual.

A crust of dry bread and a cup of water was given to Warren, and the same fare thrown on the floor beside Ivan, who did not eat it and watched anxiously to see if Warren would taste his. But the boy shook his head.

"Never mind," said the woman, slyly looking over to the door where the men were bundling some ragged garments in a big square of cloth.

"Never mind. I am sorry for you, my poor boy. Soon those brutes will take us away, but I will leave one good meal for you. I promise you that if they beat me for it you shall be decently fed for once. And I am a good cook; you shall see!"

Ivan shivered. Then as the woman turned to the fire and rattled the pans, he said sharply in English:

"Warren, do not eat!"

The three turned threateningly as he spoke, but as he made no effort to continue the speech in what was to them an unknown tongue, they once more went about their tasks. As they became interested in the tasks they were doing, Ivan spoke again.

"Warren?" he said.

Warren heard. "Yes!"

"Don't try to keep the girls if they start to take them," he said as rapidly as he could talk.

"There they go again!" said the woman "What are they up to, do you think?"

Michael went over to Warren.

"Do you want your head broken again?" he scowled. "You will get it. And you, too!" He turned to Ivan, and shouted threateningly across the room. "It will be your turn if I hear you speak again."

Ivan, who had said all he wanted to, nodded and was silent.

Soon Michael and Patro picked Ivan up and carried him to the massive bench that stood at one side of the table, and seating him there, tied his legs in a clever fashion so that he was unable to reach the bonds, he was so wedged between the bench and table. The place must once have been a public wine room, and what furniture there was of the heaviest sort.

Warren they lifted and tied in the same manner on the opposite side of the great table.

"There!" said the woman Martha. "Now you can see each other, and talk as long as you like." She looked at the men and laughed.

"Where are you going?" said Ivan in Polish.

"Well," said the woman, "I don't mind telling you in the least."

"Don't do it!" warned Patro.

"Why not? They are safe," said the woman.

"Won't your bonds hold as long as necessary? You see," she said, turning to Warren, "it will be a day or two perhaps before your friends find you. And even then I don't believe you will tell my plans. It will be too late. We are going to tame these nice little girls, and make beggars of them. Something useful, you see, instead of letting them grow up in idleness as they would if they stayed with you. We will go to Prague from here and I will give the little one to my sister. Then we will get out of this accursed country soon as we can, and get away where money comes easy to the poor war refugees. What do you think of that?" She leered close to the boy's face.

Everything was ready. The food, poisoned as Ivan knew it to be, stood temptingly between them, on the table. It was not an unpleasing meal. To Warren, who had not tasted solid food for two days, everything looked inviting. Ivan felt himself shaking with excitement. All was ready. The men unbarred the door, and the woman with a last sneering jest at the boys, picked up little Rika, while Michael lifted Elinor. The child screamed.

"Warren, don't let them take me away! Don't let them take me!" she cried over and over.

"Be a good girl! We will come for you very soon," said Ivan swiftly, as she paused for breath.

The child screamed again, and Michael wound a thick muffler across her face.

The heavy door closed with a clash. The boys heard a faint cry, and then the great key turned in the lock. They looked at each other.

"What does it all mean?" said Warren. He struggled furiously to release his feet, but gave up to sit staring at Ivan. "What does it all mean?"

"Well, for one thing, " said Ivan, "that food is poisoned." He proceeded to recount to Warren, the strange circumstance of the whispered conversation which he had so clearly overheard.

"It has saved our lives," said Warren solemnly. "I am starved and would have eaten this stuff sure as nails . Gee, what an escape! Let us work out of these ropes and get out of here. Perhaps, we can get those cutthroats before they got away from the city."

For some moments the boys both wiggled and twisted to free themselves. It was in vain. So closely were they wedged between the benches and table, and so cleverly were their feet tied with rope and pieces of board to wedge them, that it was absolutely an impossibility to release themselves. All through the night they sat there, at intervals renewing their efforts to get free, and with despair growing in their hearts. They began to realize the seriousness of the situation. When Warren's watch told them that morning had come, they found themselves looking wistfully at the food. Its scent was in their famished nostrils. Warren drew a piece of fish toward him.

"I wonder if it is all poisoned," he said.

With a cry Ivan reached out and swept the food from the table. "There!" he exclaimed, "I found myself wondering the same thing. If we die, we die - but not that way, my Warren. We will be free yet. Ivanovich does not die today."

But Warren, weakened from, his hurts, laid his head down on his arms with a groan.

Ivan looked at him pityingly. The loss of his little sister had almost crushed Warren. He who was always the leading spirit, quick and resourceful, was for the moment crushed.

Ivan did not speak. He respected the grief of his friend. He knew that soon he would be himself again, planning for success.

Late that same afternoon three Boy Scouts sauntered down the dark and twisted alley leading to the river. The section of the city was strange to them, and it was now so wrecked by the recent bombardment that the enemy themselves shunned it.

The poor creatures that had once found lodging in those dark holes of want and famine had all fled at the first gunshot; and the boys idled here and there, looking at the marks of the shots, and picking up many a queer memento of the battle.

Warsaw had fallen; but the spirit of boys is the same all the world over. In their imaginations, even while the smoke of battle still hung over the city, they had planned other and victorious battles. They had already saved Warsaw for a wonderful golden future.

As they climbed around, one of them pointed to the broken plaster on the ground.

"See!" he said. "A Scout! Two of them have been here. There are the marks of the nails in their Scout shoes."

The other boys looked. Sure enough they saw distinctly the marks of the well known Scout shoes, sold even in distant Warsaw.

"Let's follow them up," said another boy, leading the way.

It was something to do and they bent to the chase like young hounds on a fresh fox trail. Rather to their disappointment, the tracks did not double or disappear here and there. They led directly down the street. As they followed, a faint cry sounded. The boys stopped, startled.

"What's that?" whispered one.

The cry was repeated. "Someone in trouble," cried the first boy, hurrying forward.

The boy behind took a quick step, and caught him by the arm.

"Stop!" he whispered. "Don't go on! That's not a human voice."

Frozen in attitudes of astonishment, the boys stood listening with all their might.

"Pshaw!" said the tall boy, Thaddeus, in his rapid Polish. "What think you would cry like that - spirits?" He laughed.

"It might be," said the second lad doggedly. "There are spirits, of course; and when souls are set free in the violence of war they say they ever return to haunt the scene of their passing."

"Well, nobody has passed here," said Thaddous, "alive or dead. Let's go on!"

"Wait just a minute," said the second boy. "I tell you there is evil somewhere about here!"

"The street is dark and crooked enough to hold almost anything," said Thaddeus. "I am not surprised now that my father always ordered me to keep away from these streets leading to the river. They say many and many a poor wretch has been bundled down there and pushed off into the Vistula. She tells no tales, that river."

The cry was repeated. It was faint, and there was a note of pain or terror in it that chilled the listeners. Very faint and far away it was too.

"I'm going back," said the second boy.

"Go!" said Thaddeus scornfully, "Go and give up your Scout badge, and tell the chapter that while the sons of Warsaw were not afraid to meet a bloody death, you are not one of them because you think the spirits are abroad in the town.

The boy blushed.

"Come!" said Thaddeus. "I know you don't mean it. There is someone in trouble. Let us find them quickly."

Following the tracks and listening every few steps for the voices, the boys reached the place where Warren and Ivan were imprisoned. They were nearly exhausted from the cramped positions and the long fast. They had called until their throats were parched, and their voices croaked and wheezed. But as they heard the boys familiar and welcome voices sound faintly through the heavy door, new energy thrilled then and they lifted their voices together in a shout that echoed in the vaulted room. It was answered.

So thick and close fitting was the door that they could not make the listeners outside understand anything but the word "Help!" which, spoken in any language, is certain to bring response. The boys outside shouted assurances which were, also not understood, but the sound of friendly voices put now life into Warren and Ivan every moment. The great locked door was baffling; but there was plenty of heavy timbers around, and finding a sort of battering ram was a moment's work. The three went to work with a will. Blow after blow fell on the heavy door. It did not yield an inch. The lock also held firm, but the new casing was built in old and rotted wood. It gave, and with a dusty splintering the door toppled in, and the boys, springing over without a moment's hesitation, entered.

They hurried to the exhausted prisoners and cut the ropes and freed them. Both boys were so numb that it was some time before the Scouts could rub feeling into the cramped legs and feet.

Warren pointed to the floor where the pieces of food were scattered. Three dead rats lay near.

"You were right, Ivan," he said with a great shudder.

"What is it?" said the Scout who was rubbing him.

"Poison," said Warren. "Meant for us." A little at a time he told the newcomers the adventures of the past long hours.

After the blow on the bead Warren had lain unconscious for so long, and when he finally roused the darkness and dungeon-like appearance of the room so perplexed him, that he thought himself delirious. He was very dizzy, and tried to sleep, feeling that if he could lose himself, he would wake and find the whole thing a bad dream. Even when his sister came and caressed him, he did not change his mind.

But finally full consciousness came, with all the suffering of his hurts, as well as the dreadful anxiety about Elinor and Rika and the seeming hopelessness of escape.

The boys all shook their heads when Ivan broke in to tell bow he had given up the great ruby, only to be thought a thief. They listened breathlessly when he told of the strange whisper that came so clearly to his ears, and when they reached the account of the poison they scarcely breathed.

"Yon couldn't see the rats, could you?" Warren asked Ivan.

"No!" said Ivan.

"Well," said Warren, "it queered me so I thought I wouldn't say anything about it. After you threw the food off the table, I looked down and presently something slipped out of the shadow. It was the biggest rat you ever saw. Much bigger than any of those. He walked around bold as anything, and I began to think what a big fellow like that could do if a fellow got down and out. Well, it made me cold. Then he went off, and I think he told a lot of the others that there was a lot of good eats on the floor, and half a dozen of them came along, and went after that meat and stuff. And when they ate it, one by one they just went staggering around for a little as though they didn't know what ailed them, and then they fell down, and I never hope to see such agony. It was back of you, Ivan, and I thought there was no use telling you. But it is all over now, for the rats and for us too; and we can be glad you fellows found us. As soon as we can walk," he ended, "we must take this thing to headquarters. We know where to look for the girls, and they must help."

The largest Scout laughed.

"You don't know what you are talking about," he said. "You can't get help from anyone. Our people, the people of Warsaw, are so scattered, that it is the same as though they did not exist. As for the others, the enemy, they laugh. I know of one lady who lost a child - But there is no use to talk. Whatever is done - we will have to do ourselves."

"We will go down ourselves, now we know where to look, and we will take the children. We are strong, if it comes to a fight; we can still get them away.

We ourselves will rescue the children." He laughed and helped Warren to his feet. "We are Scouts," he said.

"It is a good thing we are," said another boy, busy rubbing Ivan who lay with set teeth, stifling the pain of returning circulation in his tortured ankles.

"You did a wonderful thing, Warren," he continued, addressing the boy he named, "when you started the Boy Scout movement over here. Well I remember the day I told my people about it. They were amused. They called it one of the crazy plans of the Americans. They were afraid to have me join. They were afraid that I would get into trouble with the government. Everything is so strictly watched. But they were so glad to have me have a good chance to learn the American language, that they would not quite forbid me. I thought I never would learn. Sometimes I thought I knew it well; and there would appear in your speech some strange words that you could not seem to translate to us, and you called it all with one word, 'Slang!' You said you could not get along without it. And it was and is the most difficult part of all the noble language. Yet now that I can read your native language, I never seem able to find this slang you talk in the books or magazines. I have kept a careful list of all I have heard you say, and I am teaching it to my mother and to my sister who was to have been presented at Court, had not this war come up. It would be fine for them to be able to talk this slang to your ambassador." He stopped speaking Polish, and broke into lame and halting English. "Do you get me, Lissee!" he asked.

Warren groaned.

"For the love of Mike!" he said. "No, I don't mean that! For Pete's sake - " He groaned again. "I don't know what I mean," he said, "but I do get you. Mikelovo and you don't want to teach your precious family any more gems." He hastily sought an excuse. "You see only men and boys talk it as a general thing. Better teach the women stuff out of the books."

"All right," said the earnest student of the American language, "but in all other things the Boy Scouts are all right for my family."

"When the books and other things came from your country, I showed them to my father with trembling; but he approved. And now we will do all the great things, we ourselves, that our poor country cannot do. We will help your good father, and rescue the little children."

"One thing I have noticed," said the first boy. "There are no boys around the streets giving any help to the hurt or lost or troubled except the Boy Scouts. When Warsaw rises again, there will be a great order here, and all the boys in the city shall have a chance to prepare for it."

"Gee whiz, yes," said the student of slang, solemnly, "we will get 'em all in line."

CHAPTER VII

THE CARVED PANEL

We will leave the Boy Scouts puzzling over the tremendous problem of getting in touch with headquarters and releasing Professor Morris and the others, while we visit a magnificent home far up in the residential part of the city, where the beautiful parks, wide streets and fine buildings all told of great wealth.

Many of the places lay in ruins, but here and there arose a dazzling white marble building that bad happily escaped the destruction of the iron rain that had poured over the ill-fated city. Many of these were occupied by the officers and men of the invading army. Destruction of the worst sort went with them, and the unhappy owners had, whenever possible, secreted the most valuable of their belongings. Pictures, jewels, silver, furs and even rugs were hidden in secret vaults or buried in gardens and cellars. For the people of Warsaw, as well as their fair city, were ruined, although sooner or later the scraps saved could be converted into money. Rich and poor fared alike; for the present, at least, everyone needed food and, safe shelter.

In the dining-room of one of the finest places saved from the destroying shells sat a group of officers. They were big, blonde men, and they talked roughly and rapidly in their native German. It was plain to see that they were quarreling. One of them, rising from the great carved chair in which he had been lounging, kicked it from his path and walked nervously up and down the room. He was scowling ferociously while with his saber point he jabbed little holes in the Russian leather covering the back of the chair opposite him.

He shook his head as the man who was walking up and down neared his chair.

"I tell you, Otto, you can't do it," he said. "You can't burry things so. Those people are Americans. You can't execute that old man on a bare suspicion. What if his notes are a code? We have them, at all events; and we have him; and we must wait until the General returns."

"That's not my idea at all!" scowled the other man. "This is war. I am in command, my friend, and if I think I have a spy, and see that it is my duty to stand this man up against a wall, then what? Bang! Bang! It is all over. What can be said?"

"What is your idea exactly?" asked the man at the table. "What is the use of hurrying things so? It sounds like murder to me. I think the old man is perfectly harmless. He is probably just what he claims, a professor in one. of the American Universities. I've heard of this Princeton. It is a place of some size and standing."

"That is just it, Gustav!" cried the other.

"That is one reason for suspecting him. He is too glib with his Princeton. Himmel! Did you ever hear a man talk so fast and so much and use such words? I can speak as good English as any man my age, but there were words, dozens of them, that I had never dreamed of."

"Is that the real reason why you are going to shoot him as a spy?" asked Gustav, coming back to the main point once more.

"I don't suppose I shall shoot him at all," answered Otto grimly. "I want to, that's all, but I can't do it unless I have sufficient cause, no matter how would like to remove him. He is in the way."

Gustav stared, and laid down his saber. "I See!" he said, nodding his head slowly. "The girl?"

"Yes! The girl!" said Otto. He frowned and continued to walk up and down, while the other laughed.

"What would you?" he demanded. "You would get yourself into all sorts of trouble. There is no kidnapping of young women in this campaign, remember!"

"I would like to marry her," said Otto coolly. "She is so pretty and sweet."

"So are the German girls," declared Gustav, loyally.

"What a romantic episode!" sighed Otto, rolling his eyes in a sentimental manner. "I discover this beautiful American here in Warsaw, in the heart of the war; I love her; I marry her. It is wonderful!"

"It certainly is," said Gustav. "Wonderful indeed! And in order to bring her to a proper idea of your goodness and charm, you shoot her father and brother - do you shoot her brother, by the way?"

Otto scowled. "You are coarse, my friend," he said. "I do not shoot anyone.

Germany merely destroys a spy. As for the brother, he is small, I think he disappears."

"Does the German army cause that too?" asked Gustav.

"Don't jest," said Otto. "I am in earnest."

"In truth, so am I!" answered Gustav. "You are crazy, just plain crazy. The man is no more a spy than I am, I'll be bound!"

Otto shrugged his broad shoulders. "You don't know whereof you speak," he said. "You have not heard him talk, have you?"

"No, I'll grant that," Gustav acknowledged. "Have him brought in and let me hear him."

"Very well," said Otto, "but speak English to him. His German is so bad that he ought to he shot for that if for nothing else."

He turned and summoned an orderly. The two men sat in silence. At a nearby table two lieutenants were busy writing. They did not speak but looked eagerly as the door opened, and the prisoners entered. The Lieutenants shifted in their chairs and smiled at each other in anticipation. Gustav caught their fleeting grins and dismissed them from the room with a curt command, then turned his attention to the group standing just within the door.

Professor Morris stood with a protecting arm around each of his children. He looked broken and old, and wore the air of a man who has been rudely wakened from a secure and comfortable sleep to view some unimagined horror. The War, the bombardment and the fall of Warsaw, had at last become something more than a spectacle to be transferred to the pages of his book. It was a frightful fact, a living reality in which men died by thousands, and little children perished, where women's hearts broke with their anguish and despair.

He found that War recognizes but few laws, and even fewer obligations. It seemed that his standing as a man of learning, his claim as a citizen of the United States, availed him nothing. Standing there, a prisoner, with a helpless child on either side, the ivy-covered walls of his beloved Princeton seemed far away indeed. As lie closed his tired eyes for an instant he could see a clear and lovely picture of the velvet green campus and the great iron gates opening on the smooth and level streets shaded by lofty trees. He heard the chimes, the laughter of happy young fellows passing to and fro. There were rows and rows of peaceful homes, stately mansions and simple cottages. On level, perfectly kept tennis courts, here and there, men and girls all in white played tennis. He saw his friends -

But opening his weary eyes, he saw a gorgeous, tumbled room whose princely draperies were torn and full of saber cuts, a sideboard where priceless glass had been a target for the rough play by rougher men. Before him were the two hard, blonde German faces, and there he stood, a prisoner, with his two children clinging to him. Warren and Elinor were gone, he knew not where.

Captain Handel stood motionless, but Captain Schmitt rose civilly and bowed when he saw Evelyn. He could not help it. The girl was so noble, so lovely, and hid her fright so gallantly, that he was compelled to pay her the slight courtesy that he did.

"Captain Handel tells me that this notebook is yours, Professor Morris," Gustav commenced in almost perfect English.

"It is," said the Professor. He eyed it hungrily, and reached a hand out without thinking what he did.

Gustav drew the book back.

"It has a suspicious look," he said. "So many plans and measurements and specifications. Will you not explain?"

The Professor reddened. He shut his mouth stubbornly.

"Those are private notes," be said. "I was sent over here to make what discoveries I could along certain lines."

"What, did I tell you, Gustav?" broke in Otto, turning to his brother officer and speaking in a low tone. "There is the whole thing! He was a spy sent to make discoveries along 'certain

George Durston

lines.' He confesses that. He has succeeded in doing so. The book tells us that."

"Wait, wait!" begged Gustav. "Professor Morris, do you understand that you are here facing a most serious charge?"

"It is a silly, trumped up charge," declared the Professor, irritably. "Silly trumped up charge! I absolutely will not answer your questions. Wait until you hear from the American Consul."

"We won't hear from him," said Gustav gently. "You are in our hands, bearing suspicious documents, and you refuse to answer our questions. Do you realize the seriousness of this affair?"

"Certainly not!" declared the Professor, "and let me tell you, my young friend, I shall write this thing up in the papers when I return to America. I shall make public your personal attitude in the matter. At the present all I demand is release and that manuscript on the table beside you. Also my notebook." He bowed slightly and stood waiting as though he fully expected the officers to do his bidding, as indeed he did.

"Will you explain your notes?" asked Gustav quietly.

Otto was nervously biting his small moustache, his eyes fixed on Evelyn's lovely face.

"No! No!" cried the Professor loudly, "a thousand times no! I refuse to share with you the results of my researches. What, and have you get the credit of all my labor? Never!" He clenched his hands.

"Father - " began Evelyn pleadingly.

"Be silent, Evelyn!" commanded her father sternly. "I know what I am about! I refuse to say anything, whatever happens."

"You had better think this over, Professor," said Gustav. "We will leave you here alone for half an hour. Talk it over with your children and decide if you wish to give up your life for the sake of these notes. Explain them to us, and we will promise you safe conduct out of the country. The girl and boy will have to remain as guarantee of your good faith. They will not he harmed. In case you will not do as we suggest - " He tapped his saber, and started to the door.

Otto spoke abruptly.

"The windows are barred," he said. "Two men guard the door. You cannot escape. Decide!"

He looked longingly at Evelyn and followed Gustav from the room. The heavy door shut silently behind them but not before they had a glimpse of the two soldiers standing at attention in the hallway.

While they stood looking at it, it opened and Otto entered, closing it after him.

"I may as well tell you," he said. "You will shoot as a spy if you do not explain your charts and figures and leave the country."

Then as though he could not conceal his triumph, he added, "In any case, you know your daughter remains here."

"Remains here?" cried the Professor. "How is that? What do you mean?"

Otto shrugged his shoulders.

"I like her," he said coolly. "I might marry her. You are very lovely," he added, turning his bold, cold eyes on Evelyn.

She hid her face against her father's shoulder.

Otto laughed.

Jack sprang at him with a shrill cry. The big man caught the boy, and flung him contemptuously to the floor.

"Be careful, little sparrow!" he said. "A second time and I will crush you! I'm going now," he said, turning to the Professor. "In half an hour we will come and you will tell us which you prefer - death or safe conduct." He bowed. "Good-bye for a little, Mees Evelyn, he said and closed the door behind him.

Evelyn threw herself on her father's shoulder and burst into sobs. "Oh, father, father, what shall we do?" she cried.

The Professor was silent, then he said, "Well, my dear, I actually believe that young man meant what he said."

"Of course he did!" sobbed Evelyn.

"In that ease," said the Professor firmly, "I would as lief be dead as to have the work of a lifetime destroyed by those rascals."

He hastened to the table and took up the portfolio enclosing his book. "It's all here," he said after a glance.

"But father, whatever they do to you, they are going to keep me here. What will I do? What will I do?"

She ran to the windows and looked out. It was just as they had been told. The casements were heavily barred and there was but one door, the one through which the officers had passed. The walls were paneled half way up with old oak. The room was solid as a dungeon. There was not a chance for escape. In a few minutes the soldiers would return and tear her father from her.

Her father was speaking. She listened.

"All here," he said, "every page! That is fortunate indeed."

He looked searchingly at Evelyn. "I have a plan, my," he said. "This is a very dreadful affair, but on second thought a scheme occurs to me. I will explain somewhat of my notes, but not enough so they could amplify them. Then, with my safe conduct, I will go over to Germany, explain the whole affair, and demand your release. You will doubtless be absolutely safe here, absolutely safe. This young Handel seems rather a rattle-brained youth, but Captain Schmitt looked conservative and sane. I will place you in his Charge. John is with you, and you will be perfectly safe, I am positive."

Evelyn grew deathly pale. She kissed her father's cheek, then listlessly approached the table. A revolver was lying there.

"Yes, I know that I will be safe," she said firmly. She took the weapon in her hand and looked up.

As she raised her eyes, she looked straight into the face of a girl about her own age, who stood motionless against the wall, one hand outstretched its though to call her. Evelyn stared in unbelief. An instant before they had been alone in the room! Were her senses leaving her? She looked at her father and brother. They, too, were staring, speechless and wild-eyed. So she did not imagine the graceful figure and lovely face with its dark troubled eyes.

The stranger pressed a finger on her lips in a gesture of silence, then she beckoned, and as they approached, tiptoeing over the thick rug, she turned and pressed a finger on a carved rosette in the oak panel. Without a sound it slid open, and they found themselves in a narrow, stone passage. Once more the strange girl motioned for silence. Then she slid an iron grating across the secret door through which they had come, and turning ran lightly down the passage. Without a moment's hesitation, Evelyn started after, her hand still clasping the revolver which she had taken from the table. The Professor, clutching his recovered manuscript, followed, while Jack brought up the rear.

As they turned a corner, a faint shout reached them. The officers had returned to the empty room!

The way was long, with many sharp turns. It seemed to be a space between rooms. Once or twice shouts and laughter were faintly heard, as they seemed to pass near a room full of soldiers. It was dark. The girl ahead felt in her pocket, and brought out a tiny flashlight. They came finally to a steep flight of stairs.

Now for the first time the girl spoke. In a cautious whisper she said, "Be careful!" and holding the flash behind her for their guidance, went swiftly and lightly down, with the manner of one who is familiar with every inch of the way. The stairs were wide and shallow. There were a great many of them and they seemed to go down a long way. Evelyn wondered if the place was built on a hillside, making it a long way to the underground regions she suspected beyond or below. She afterwards found out that this was correct. A door barred with iron was at the foot of the stairs. Indeed, they ended right against it. The girl pushed the door open, and when they had entered, closed it behind them and dropped a massive bar across it. They were in a large, stone chamber, empty save for a few scraps of furniture.

Their guide swiftly crossed the room and opened another forbidding looking door. The second room was like the first, but was filled with casks and huge barrels. Beyond this again they entered a narrow passage, so very narrow that their garments brushed the walls at either side. The stones underfoot were rough and uneven.

Professor Morris walked carefully, picking his steps by the aid of the flashlight. Evelyn and Jack, more careless, stumbled frequently, but still the girl, light as a feather, flitted on, swift and sure footed.

Once more the flash revealed a wall ahead. As she approached it the girl turned and smiled. Evelyn stared. There was no sign of any opening in the rough wall and the great stones seemed fast in their cement, but the girl, stooping, pressed a corner of one of the paving stones. To their amazement it slid from its place, revealing another very narrow flight of steps. The girl descended, and when they were all down, pressed another spring, and the stone slid in place. Another flight of steps exactly like the ones they had just descended rose against the flooring; and when the girl had led the way, they one by one stepped into a large and brightly lighted room.

Professor Morris blinked; Jack turned red; Evelyn gasped with surprise.

CHAPTER VIII

THE SECRET CHAMBER

It was a vast apartment of stone, but the rugged walls were nearly covered with the most rare and beautiful hangings - curtains, tapestries and strange oriental rugs. Numerous paintings apparently of great value also hung about, or stood on the floor leaning against the wall. The stone floor was deep with rugs and fine furs. A number of couches, wide and comfortable, were set here and there, and one corner of the room was hidden by a great black and gold screen. From this corner came the comforting odor of coffee.

Professor Morris sniffed it with joy.

In the center of the ceiling hung a simple drop light of great power illuminating the place with almost the glare of sunlight. Beneath the light stood a large table littered with magazines, papers and articles of value. Beside it, in a deep easy chair, sat a woman. She was about forty years of age and beautiful. Her garments were very rich, and she sat listlessly leaning her head on her hand for she had been weeping. At her side, evidently bent on comforting her mistress, knelt a woman in the costume of a servant. A footman in livery stood at attention behind her chair. Even in that strange, sunless, underground place, everything in sight, confused though it was, gave evidence of immense wealth and luxury.

After the dark, blank, twisted passages, and the horrors so

lately escaped in the room above them, the scene seemed unreal enough to be a dream. As they appeared through the small square in the floor and stood in a hesitating group the lady in the easy chair leaned forward and looked at them earnestly.

Their guide, the young girl, pressed the spring that replaced the flagstone, and as soon as she was sure that it was adjusted, ran eagerly across the wide space and knelt at the lady's knee. She spoke rapidly and excitedly in Polish. Evelyn could catch a word occasionally. Then the lady rose and advanced with a graceful gesture of welcome.

"You are indeed welcome," she said easily in English. "I cannot be thankful enough that my daughter overheard those brutal soldiers and was able to rescue you. Come and tell me about it."

Professor Morris bowed low over the hand extended him. Then leading the way, the lady returned to the table where the footman drew chairs for the group.

Professor Morris told his story of the arrest and imprisonment and the result of the conference in the dining-room. The lady shuddered.

"You are safe now, at least," she assured him when the story was finished. "And we are happy .to have you with us. It is a comfort to have someone with whom to share one's sorrows. One has no happiness to share now." She smiled sadly.

"I am the Princess Olga Nicholani; with my husband and children I have lived here all my life. The Prince is with his troops, living or dead I know not. Our son is with him. When the war separated us I, Modjeska here and my baby girl, with a few of our old servants, remained in Warsaw.

"We were perfectly safe until the bombardment of the city commenced. Then we decided to escape, if possible. We clothed ourselves plainly, and under cover of darkness crept from the house the first night. All lights were out, and we reached the corner safely. We had planned to go down to the river front, where we had a motor boat, in which we planned to escape. But just as we turned into the river street, we were met by a maddened crowd of citizens all rushing to safety. They met us like a great wave. Modjeska and the servants were crushed against a building, but I was thrown down and for a moment stunned. When the crowd had passed, my people assisted me to consciousness, but oh, my heart - my heart! How can I tell?"

She bid her face in her hands and shuddered. Modjeska clasped her in. other in her arms, murmuring loving words of comfort.

In a moment the Princess looked up.

"You can imagine our agony, Professor Morris, when we found that our baby was gone. She had been torn from me in the crowd. We could not find her. We searched all night. Then they brought me home here by a secret passage, and, the men hastened to bring down everything movable of value or comfort. We have plenty of light because we have our own electric light system, and this building was not struck by shell or bomb.

"The secret passage through which Modjeska brought you was revealed to me by my husband, the Prince. His father had taught him the way, and not long before the war we carefully taught our two elder children the secret springs and all the turnings. I do not know why Modjeska happened to venture along those dark passages to the dining-room."

"I don't know either, mother," said Modjeska, shyly. "I had a strange feeling that I had to go. Something seemed to drag me there."

"Did you hear the conversation?" asked Professor Morris.

"Part of it," answered Modjeska. "Enough to tell me that something terrible was going on. I was wild with fright. I did not know how I could help you until I heard that dreadful man say that he and the other officer would go out for half an hour. And mother, he told them they could not escape, because the windows were barred, and the door guarded. Then at first, when I pressed the spring, the panel would not open. Something had rusted. I worked and worked before it slid, back."

"A moment later would have been too late," said the Professor, shaking his head.

"This room is absolutely safe," said the Princess. "There are seven or eight of these chambers, about fifty feet from the house, under the garden. So compose yourselves and rest. I cannot leave - half the city is searching for my baby - I can do nothing but sit here in agony and pray for her return. I know she is dead; I almost pray that she is, but how can I ever rest until I know?" She bent her head and sobbed.

Professor Morris cleared his throat.

"I do not doubt that the infant is safe, Madame. No one would deliberately molest a helpless baby. "

"She wasn't really a baby," said Modjeska. "Mother calls her that because she was so tiny. She could walk, and talk a little too."

"Don't say was!" cried the Princess. "Don't talk as if she was dead!"

"No, mother darling, no!" soothed the girl.

"How old is she?" asked Evelyn.

The Princess again controlled herself. "Rika -"

She had no chance to continue -

"Rika?" cried Professor Morris, and Evelyn, and Jack, and again, "Rika?"

Evelyn reached inside her blouse, and pulled out a heavy gold chain hung with a splendid diamond ornament.

"Is this yours?" she cried.

The Princess took one look, then seized Evelyn by the shoulders.

"Yes! Yes!" she cried, chokingly. "Tell me where is she? Have you seen my baby? Tell me! Tell me!"

Evelyn said the thing quickest.

"She is with my sister, and I think they are safe," she cried.

The Princess gave a deep sigh and fainted quietly away.

It was a long time before she recovered, and then she wanted to be told over and over all about little Rika. How she had looked, how she had borne the separation, everything. The Morrises having been assured by Ivan that Warren was on the track of the men who had kidnapped the children, and knowing the cleverness and determination that Warren always put into everything he ever did, were positive that Warren had the children safely in his possession. And Evelyn knew well that once with him, they would not get out of his sight again. All of this she used to comfort the Princess who could scarcely contain herself for joy.

"Now it will all come out right!" she said. "When the men come back next time, we can set them to hunting up your son and Prince Ivan, and we will soon be reunited."

She clapped her hands softly, and the footman approached.

"Luncheon, Michael!" she said, and the Professor watched with pleasure the speed with which the Princess was obeyed. Soon they were eating a delicious and much needed meal. The Princess herself was so strengthened by the tonic of hope and joy that she was able to enjoy the delicate food. She could not hear enough about Rika and at every sound declared that the men must be returning, although Modjeska reminded her over and over that they were unlikely to return before dark.

The afternoon wore on, Professor Morris and Evelyn glad to rest after the recent shocks, and Jack playing games with Modjeska, while the Princess walked restlessly about the vast chamber, constantly looking at her watch. Finally she said joyfully:

"It must be growing dark now. The men will soon return, and we will send them to your house where the boys and your little daughter will be waiting with my baby Rika. Oh, how can I ever be thankful enough to you for your goodness to her?"

Professor Morris smiled. "Considering the fact that Miss Modjeska has saved all our lives," he said, "I think that you need feel under no obligations to us. We were delighted to entertain the little Rika. I am positive that my son will have them in safety somewhere, so you really need not worry. I do not."

Evelyn suppressed a smile. She was quite sure her father did not worry. He was always ready to let someone else do the worrying for him.

Suddenly a silver knob fastened to the wall dropped from its place and swung back and forth on a thin chain.

"They have come!" cried the Princess. She rushed across the room, and as the footman drew aside one of the heavy hangings, she pressed with all her might on a rough spot in the granite wall. As in the case of the flooring, the wall itself parted and slowly swung open. In the dark opening stood not one of the well-known house servants, but a slight figure covered with dirt and grime. He was tattered and barefooted. Under the dirt his pallid face looked deathly, but fire blazed in the dark eyes, the fire of love.

"Mother!" he cried. "Don't you know me?"

The Princess gave a cry, and clasped her son in a passionate embrace.

"Ignace!" she cried; and "Ignace!" over and over, while she patted him and felt of him as though to assure herself that it was not a dream.

"Where is your father, Ignace?" she whispered finally, as a dreadful thought pierced her.

"I come from him," said the young man wearily. "He is wounded, mother, and needs you, but be brave, because he will live. Let me sit while I tell you."

He sank wearily into a chair, still clinging to the hand of the Princess. He paid no attention to the strangers, but closed his eyes.

"I thought I would never see you again, dear ones," he said huskily. "I simply can't tell you now what we have been through. All I can say is that in the final encounter, as the enemy passed Lodz, my dear father was desperately wounded. I missed him, and searched for him. When I found him he was unconscious. Mother, I thought he was dead. But he lived, and under cover of darkness we carried him to the house of our Aunt Francoise. She has turned it into a hospital, mother, and all the forty rooms are filled with soldiers. Well, father had good care then, for all the rush Aunt Francoise had him taken to the hidden chapel in the east wall, and it is quiet and safe. But you must come and care for him, mother, for there are not enough nurses by half, and the men suffer so."

"Where was he injured, Ignaee?" asked the Princess, shuddering. The boy hesitated.

"Mother dear, it is pretty bad, but I have see it so much worse. He has lost his left arm."

The Princess covered her eyes. "Oh, my dear, my dear!" she murmured. "How can I bear this for you?"

"It might be far worse," said Ignace cheerily. "We must start back to him tonight. Did you save any of the motor cars?" He turned to Michael.

"Two, your Excellency," said the man. "They are hidden in a haystack down past the woods at the end of the estate. The large touring car, and your racer."

"Good!" said Ignace; then suddenly, "Where is my little Rika?"

At once the Princess and Modjeska commenced the story of her loss, and all the other events leading up to the appearance of the Morrises and the strange coincidence of their having found the little girl.

Ignace listened breathlessly.

Once more the silver knob fell. Someone else was coming.

The footman opened the stone portal, and three men entered. They bowed profoundly to the Princess and greeted Ignace with deepest respect.

They had of course no news of Rika but the Princess was able to impart the good news to them and to tell them that, after they had eaten, they could go to the Morris house and fetch the two girls, Ivan and Warren back.

"I am not sure that we can do so tonight, Excellency," one said.

"There is great confusion in the house. A triple guard surrounds it. So far the guards are no nearer than our doorway, but if they spread their lines we will not be able to get back. I heard a soldier say that two important prisoners had slipped out from under the very eyes of the officers and could not be found. They are in hiding somewhere, and every effort is being made to find them. They know they have not left the building."

He glanced suspiciously at the strangers.

"Yes, they are here," said the Princess. In a few words she explained. The man bowed low.

"By your leave, Excellency, I will take the others and go - at once," he said. "One may eat some other time perhaps. We are in danger even here, and I will not feel safe until we are on our way."

"Go then by all means," said Ignace. "He is quite right, mother, and the sooner we are out of this, the better."

"Go, and in the meantime we will prepare for the journey."

The men saluted and left silently, and the Princess with the woman-servant and the two girls, collected dark cloaks and warm rugs. A bountiful lunch was prepared and packed.

Professor Morris, holding his manuscript, sat searching through one pocket after another with a mournful persistence. Finally Evelyn noted him and asked what was the matter.

"I have lost my reading glasses," he said.

"Can't we find them for you?" asked Modjeska politely. She started to look on the rugs.

"They are not here," said the Professor. "I heard the ease fall out of my pocket when we were coming through the passage."

"Then we will get them," said Modjeska. "It will only take a minute. Would you like to come with me, Evelyn?"

"Yes, I would!" said Evelyn, who was nervous and wanted to do something.

"Hurry!" said the Princess. "I know it is absolutely safe, but I can't bear one of you out of my sight for a moment."

The passage was very cold and damp, and the girls each put on a heavy, dark cloak. They threaded their way through the rooms that lay between the living- room and the passage, and went up the narrow hallway with the flashlight illuminating the stone floor. The case was found at last and they were turning to go back, when the sound of an explosion reached their ears and a dim light appeared at the end of the corridor. For a moment the girls stood motionless; then they turned, and ran swiftly down the twisted way to the sliding stone, and found themselves once more in the room they had left, but it was in darkness.

The electric lights were out and the little flashlights made but a dim illumination in the room.

The men had returned, and all stood staring as the two girls raced into the room and told their story.

"I think they are dynamiting the dining-room to find the prisoners. We must leave now," cried Ignace. "No one knows how they may guard the grounds. They are bound to find their victims."

"'Where is Rika?" cried Modjeska.

"They could find no trace of any of them," said the Princess. "We can only hope that the boys have taken the little girls either to the American Consul's or away from Warsaw. We will have to trust to them and believe that they are all together, until we can get in touch with them. In the meantime there is but one course open. We must go to the Prince at Lodz."

"And at once, mother! I have a feeling that we are not safe even here. Have you your jewels?"

"I have them all," said the Princess. "All that I had placed on Rika, and which Miss Evelyn has returned, and the court jewels as well.

"Then let us go," said Ignace. "I'll lead the way, Jan. When we reach the waterfall, go ahead and see if all is safe."

In perfect silence they left the room, slipping along a narrow, low passageway that at first seemed walled with stone, then gave forth a moldy, earthy odor.

Presently they heard the sound of gently falling water, and found themselves under a narrow waterfall. Again a clever spring was touched by some hand in the darkness, and one by one they emerged so close to the edge of the falling water that the spray wet them.

They were in the open air once more.

Ignace clasped Evelyn by the hand, and she could feel the nervous strain in his grasp. Noiseless as shadows, they slid from tree to tree through the great park, and down the grove of interlacing trees. It was a long walk. As Evelyn was wondering if she could possibly go much further, a dark, round shape appeared in the opening ahead.

It was the haystack.

CHAPTER IX

NEW CLUES

Walking along in the pleasant, fresh air, Warren and Ivan soon gained control of their cramped muscles. It was good to be free. They were faint from lack of food, however, and at the suggestion of one of the Boy Scouts, retraced their steps to the deserted bakery and once more raided the ovens. Then, rested and refreshed, they picked their way into the residential section where they knew the officers of the invading forces had settled themselves.

Repeated questions finally led them to the building where Professor Morris and his son and daughter had been taken as spies. As they approached it, they noticed a triple guard at the gate and a large number of soldiers close around the palace. The boys hesitated.

"Let's see what this all means," said Ivan. "There is some special reason for all these soldiers on guard. Perhaps we can get one of them to talk."

"They are not allowed to, you know," said Warren.

"We will try this," said Ivan. He took a large cake from his pocket and approached the nearest soldier. He was a young fellow with a wistful, hungry face, and as Ivan approached, his keen eyes fastened themselves on the bread.

George Durston

"Eat?" said Ivan.

"Yes," said the soldier, seizing the cake and biting off a great corner of it. "Bless you, brother, I was starving!"

"There is more where that came from," said Ivan. "If you are hungry, why don't you go eat your supper."

"Eat?" said the soldier bitterly. "Who knows how many hours we have been on guard here? I guarded a door in there all day, and now they have sent me here. The Captain is so enraged that he thinks nothing of us, nothing!"

Ivan leaned carelessly against the wall and shrugged his shoulders.

"What happened?" he asked, idly.

The soldier laughed. "It is funny," he said. "You are nothing but a boy, so it will not hurt to talk to you, and I have been silent so long that my tongue's stiff. Besides, this is good cake. Well, know then, little brother, that some people were brought here last night with suspicious papers on them. An old man, a boy and a beautiful girl. The old man would not explain the mysterious words in his little book, and they threatened him with death. He did not believe it. Did I tell you he was an American? He was. These Americans never fear. They say simply, "Kill me? That is impossible. Postpone it, if you please, while I write to the Consul!" Always it is so. Well, that old man, he could not be made to realize that Captain Handel is absolute ruler now, right here. They were brought to the state dining-room this morning, and the Captain told them straight what he intended to do. It was death for the old man and the boy, and he would spare the girl." The soldier laughed. "I and one other were guarding the door, so we heard. Presently the two Captains came out. As they left the room Captain Handel called back, 'Half an hour. Just half an hour, understand!'

"Then he closed the door sharply. The two Captains went to a little table not far from the door, and sat down. They were not for one second out of sight of the door.

"We two stood directly facing it about three feet away in the hall.

"The half hour passed., Captain Handel looked every minute at his watch, and Captain Schmitt kept saying, 'Wait, wait; be fair.'

"At last the time was up. They went to the door. Captain Schmitt straightened his saber belt, and threw the door wide.

"He looked, then he dashed in, almost upsetting Captain Handel. The room was empty. We could see. He called us, and together we searched in and on and under everything in the great room. We rapped on the wall. We examined the iron bars, but the windows had not even been opened.

"Captain Handel went into a fearful rage. The prisoners had disappeared as though they had never been. Even the book was gone from the table, and the package of papers the old man had guarded.

"We went over every foot of the place again and again. There was not an inch that sounded hollow, as though there was a secret passage. We even tore out a panel of the woodwork, and found a stone wall behind it."

The soldier finished his cake, and drew a grimy hand across his lip.

"That was good, brother," he said.

"What happened then?" asked Ivan, while Warren pressed closer.

"Why, we hunted all day," said the soldier, "but of course we couldn't find them. Why should we?"

"Why not?" asked Ivan.

"Why not?" repeated the soldier. "Why, those were not human beings at all. The old man was too silly for a real man, the girl was too beautiful. Human beings do not disappear from a guarded room with four stone walls about it."

The man lowered his voice, and spoke in a whisper. "They were devils, of course," he said.

The boys were silent.

"Of course," said the soldier, "Captain Handel would not believe anything so simple. He would not believe they were gone, so tonight he fixed them. It is all over now, and I wish I could go get some supper."

"What did he do?" asked Ivan, trying to keep the anxiety out of his voice.

"He dynamited the room," said the soldier calmly. "That part of the palace is in ruins. The stones fell like rain. No human being could have lived in it.

But they did not find the bodies. However, they may be buried under the wreckage. I don't believe it, though." He sighed. "That was good cake," he said.

"Here's another," said Warren. He clutched Ivan and sunk into the shadow. He was shaking.

"It is all over, Ivan," he whispered. "They have killed them."

Ivan pondered. "I don't know," he said finally. "One thing is sure, if all those soldiers could not find them, it is certain we can't. They are either safe, Warren, or else they are where we can never help them any more. It seems to me that the only thing to do now is to go straight to Lodz and find Elinor."

"Yes, that is the only thing to do," said Warren. "If I let myself think about Evelyn, I will go mad. We will go to Lodz."

"How?" asked Ivan.

"We will have to walk," replied Warren.

"Well, I hope we can get a lift someway or other," said Ivan. "At any rate, we must get out of this. I know every step of this part of the city. This place belongs to Prince Nicholani. I used to play all the time in this park."

He led the way rapidly through the beautiful grounds and entered a grove of noble trees. They went on and on through the shadows, until they reached the open fields. Beside the highway a great pile of hay lay scattered.

"We might sleep here for the rest of the night," Ivan suggested.

"Not if you can go on," said Warren. "I think we had better get as far from the city as possible."

"Very well," said Ivan, "but let us rest for half an hour."

They flung themselves on the hay, and in a moment Ivan was asleep. Warren could not rest, however, and sat staring moodily into the night. In half an hour he roused his friend, and they started onward. They proceeded in silence, each busily thinking, Warren trying to bear up and take his blows manfully, and Ivan at a loss to know what to say to the brave boy who had lost all he held dear in so terrible a manner.

The road was level, and they went rapidly. As they rounded a sharp turn, they saw an automobile ahead of them. It was a low racing car and stood at the side of the road. There was some trouble on, for a couple of men were bending over a wheel.

"They have had a puncture," exclaimed Warren, "and they are

headed toward Lodz. Let's see if they will give us a lift."

He boldly approached the men, who started, then looked relieved to see that it was a couple of boys.

"What's the trouble?" said Warren in Polish. The main straightened, and threw his hands up in a gesture of despair. "All the trouble in the world!" he exclaimed. "The tire is punctured, and I cannot mend it. I am not a chauffeur, but I can drive this ear a little, and my master told me to bring it to him. I don't know what to do. Of course, as soon as it comes light the soldiers will seize it."

"I can fix the tire," said Warren. "I know all about it, but we are going to Lodz and we ought not to wait. It is a long way."

"Good!" said the man. "We are going to Lodz, too. There are only two seats, but we will carry you somehow. Only be quick and mend the fire. Our lives may depend on it."

Warren turned the light on the wheel and went to work. He had always prided himself on his swiftness in working out tire troubles, and when he saw the bad tear in the tube, he took it off and replaced it with one of the new tires strapped to the rear of the machine. He worked in desperate haste, and Ivan, at his side, worked with equal desperation.

The men watched or restlessly walked up and down the road talking in undertones to each other. It was evident that their knowledge of cars was but slight, and they were forced to trust to the young stranger if they were to proceed at all on their perilous journey.

When the tire was in place and pumped up, Warren hastily collected the tools and started to replace them in the tool box but Ivan stopped him with a word. He spoke sharply to the men.

"Take these things," he said. "We are ready!"

The man who had spoken first took the wheel, and his companion the other seat. Ivan sat on his knee, with Warren on the running board.

It was soon evident that there was something wrong. The car went plowing along on low speed, the engine bucking and starting.

"Good heavens, Ivan!" exclaimed Warren, after a few miles of this jerky progress. "What ails the thing? Do you suppose the dub knows how to drive?"

Ivan turned to the man at the wheel.

"What's the matter?" he asked. "Do you know how to drive? What ails the car?"

"I don't know," said the man. "In truth I have never driven but twice, but I thought I could and when the Princess told me to bring this car after her I was sure I could. She is ahead with her son and Princess Modjeska and some guests. I fear I will not be able to reach Lodz." He pressed a lever at random, and the ear shot forward with a speed that nearly threw Warren from the step. Another frantic attempt and she slowed down with a suddenness that almost put the others through the wind shield.

"Here, stop!" commanded Warren. "Get out of that seat and let me drive! Ivan, tell him I simply eat cars!"

The machine stopped, and the Man thankfully resigned his seat to Warren, who drew up the heavy motor gloves, and settled himself in his seat. The car, a beautiful French model, was familiar to Warren, and he pressed the starter with perfect confidence. And he was justified. Like a swallow, the beautiful machine skimmed the smooth and level road, leaving Warsaw with all its tragedy and far behind.

Warren had scarcely slept for two nights. He had had but little food, and his bandaged head felt light and strange. As they went on and on, Warren commenced to wonder if he could possibly make the distant city. At intervals strange colored lights flashed before his eyes, and faint, booming noises sounded in his ears.

They had not encountered a soul. It was as though the whole country, after its terrible conflict, lay dead. Finally a faint streak of gray appeared in the east. Dawn was coming.

"How far to Lodz?" he called. "Just over the hill?"

"Just over yonder hill," said the man at his side.

Warren slowed down, and dropped one tired hand from the wheel.

"Where are you going when you get to the city?" he inquired.

"If we get through," the man replied, "I am to go to the palace where lives a sister of our Princess. She has turned it into a hospital. By a strange chance, our Prince was taken there when he was wounded. The Princess must, be there now.'

"Very well," said Warren. "Direct me when we reach the city."

It grew brighter, and was quite light when they entered the quiet streets. Fortunately they were not stopped, and with the guidance of the man beside him Warren drew safely up before the wide stone steps of the palace.

The car stopped. Warren shut off the engine, and the others jumped out, glad to stretch themselves. Warren alone made no effort to move. The others after stamping their cramped legs, turned to look at him.

His hand was still on the wheel, but he was unconscious.

They carried him into the great hall, and a nurse in uniform directed them to an empty cot and hurried after a doctor. He pronounced it simply a case of exhaustion, and gave orders which the nurse rapidly filled, motioning the others to leave as she did so.

The servants turned to Ivan and thanked him for his assistance. For a moment Ivan thought that it would be a good plan to go to the Princess, and tell her that he was in Lodz. Then he decided that the presence of a boy in the city, although he was the son of her very good friend, would only cause her to feel responsible for his welfare or safety; so he merely nodded, turned his back to tell the nurse that he would return shortly, and then he walked listlessly down into the heart of the town.

Hucksters were driving into the open market. Doors were opening here and there. A company of soldiers passed at double quick. Ivan wondered where they were going. He wondered, too, what possible chance he had to get something to Pat.

There were no Scouts in Lodz besides his tired self and the exhausted boy back in the hospital cot. Ivan thought of Warren with a gratitude that he could not have put in words. Warren had taught him so many things. With Boy Scout principles and Boy Scout training, he had changed from a haughty, helpless young aristocrat to a helpful, well-balanced boy, perfectly capable of taking care of himself and of assisting others as well. Ivan felt the change; he was so reliant, so strong. A few months ago, he would have stood helpless in his present situation, conscious only that he was Prince Ivan Ivanovich and must be looked after. Now, as he faced the morning light, hungry, ragged, and with only the American nickel in his pocket, he smiled at fate and went on without fear to enter whatever adventure might come.

The only thing that worried him was the want of enough money to buy himself a bit of bread and a dried fish. He reflected that he could easily have asked the Princess for enough to supply his wants, but he would not turn back.

Ahead of him, an old man with a heavily laden cart was having trouble with a skittish horse. In vain he pulled on the lines. In vain he threatened and coaxed. The young creature would not stand, and while the old man worried with it, vegetables and long sticks of black bread were slyly stolen out of the end of his cart. Ivan approached.

"Let me hold the horse, father," he said, taking it by the bridle as he spoke.

The old man threw his hands up in a gesture of thankfulness.

"Blessings on you, my son!" he cried. "These thieves will ruin me while I speak with that foolish animal. Hold fast, my son, and I will give you your breakfast."

Ivan nodded, and the old man turned eagerly to his customers.

Presently he reached over, and handed Ivan a generous pie6e of bread and some fresh fruit. Ivan watched the throngs as he ate, holding the horse with his left hand, although it was now perfectly quiet.

As he idly watched the persons passing, he noted that with the passing time, the market had become crowded. People moved in throngs.

And then, as the crowd before him happened to part, Ivan noticed in the distance a woman hurrying away. She had a big basket on her arm, filled with provisions. A little girl clung to her other hand. She was ragged, dirty and pale; but Ivan recognized Elinor.

Dropping the horse's rein, he dashed toward them, but the crowd had closed, and he was too late. The earth seemed to have swallowed them. Like a hound on a trail, he searched the market over and over, but not a trace could he find of the woman or child. In his surprise at seeing, Elinor, he had failed to take particular notice of the woman. But as he thought of it, he felt that, it was not the one he had seen in Warsaw and be remembered that that woman bad spoken of her sister in Lodz.

Feeling that there was nothing to be gained by remaining longer in the market, Ivan hurried back to the hospital, where he found Warren much better, and fretting because he was not allowed to get up.

"Well, I've seen Elinor!" said Ivan, as soon as he entered the ward.

Warren sat up, his eyes bulging under, his bandage.

"Have you, honest?" he cried. "Where is she?"

"Well, I lost her in the crowd," said Ivan, and told the whole story.

Warren lay listening carefully.

"Well, as long as we know she is here in the same town, we know we will find her. And there won't be any slip the next time." His face clouded. "But, Ivan," he said huskily, "I can't bear to think of my dear Evelyn, and poor father, and little Jack." He closed his lips and shut his eyes in a desperate effort to control his grief.

Warren's cot was drawn across a closed door. And on the other side of that door sat Evelyn, crying her heart out for her lost brother and sister!

CHAPTER X

BEGGARS

When poor little Elinor found herself dragged forcibly from her brother and away from the comparative safety of the underground room where Warren and Ivan had so mysteriously appeared, as she thought, to get her and take her home, her childish heart was filled with a terror so overwhelming that she did not know what she did. Notwithstanding the efforts of the woman who held her, she screamed as hard as she could and stiffened in the woman's brutal grasp until she was obliged to put her down. Elinor tried to run, but she was too tightly held. Then with a muttered rush of comments, the woman rained blows on the poor little shoulders and body until the child sank to the ground, nearly stunned from the force of the blows. Her cries died, and she lay gasping.

"Now will you be silent?" demanded the fury, shaking her. "You just try that again! Just try it, and see what I will do to you." She overwhelmed the fallen child with terrible threats until Elinor was silenced and shook as though in a chill.

"Now you had better do as I tell you," the woman said. "You will never see your brother again, never; never! And you will have to live with me, and do as I say." She jerked the child to her feet and dragged her down the street after the two men who had gone on, one of them carrying Rika.

She was still muttering when she reached them.

"This one has got to be trained," she said savagely; "and I might as well begin it right off."

Michael shrugged his shoulders. "Why don't you show a little, mercy at the first?" he inquired carelessly. "It doesn't matter to me, but I tell you, Martha, you will spoil her for everything if you handle her too roughly. She will die. I've seen her sort before."

"Then let her die!" said the woman. "Good riddance it will be if she does not take kindly to my tasks."

"Suit yourself," said Michael; "but take my advice and give her a little time."

"Time!" said Martha. "Time! What are you thinking of? There is no time! She has lost two years, as it is. You don't seem to remember, Michael, that I am as good a pickpocket as there is in Europe. That child is almost too old to begin to learn the art. The other one, Rika, is just about right; and she has such fine, delicate, little fingers. Well, this one has good hands too. But you know well that they are clumsy after they reach five. Do you remember the yellow-haired child I trained about ten years ago? Ali, she was a wonder! But you never could keep her down. How I used to beat her! She would be black welts from her shoulders to her knees. No, you could not keep her down. She was so ambitious. If she had only kept out of politics, she might have been stealing yet. But now she is in Siberia, in the mines. Bah! A home life for me, I say! What care I who is in power, so long as pretty ladies carry shopping bags and wear sparkling bracelets and flashing brooches! I say a woman wants to keep to her own place. Isn't it so, my Michael?"

"Yes, indeed, " said Michael heartily. "I read the other day - "

"Read!" said Martha scornfully. "That's another mistake. Why should a man like you read? Sooner or later it will get you in trouble. You never know what the reading may contain. Better not know. What you don't know won't hurt you."

"You are wrong," said Michael stubbornly. "Sometimes what you don't know does hurt you. If I could live again, I would be a better man. When I was a boy there was no learning to be had, except for the upper class and the priests. Now when I am old and it is too late, you can learn everything. I have loitered around the schools and listened to the boys talking their lessons over. It is amazing what they know. Why, they know everything! And there are schools where they are set to work at all sorts of trades. I took a job cleaning floors once so that I might go in and see what it was they did. Martha, those boys (they were quite little ones, too) made such beautiful things - furniture and all that. There was one little chair that you could set on your hand. It was as perfect as though it was big enough for you. I thought that I would steal it. Then I thought how sad the little fellow who made it would feel. The janitor told me there were prizes for the best workmen, and I knew that chair was best. So I didn't take it. I never wanted anything more, in my life!"

"Silly," said Martha. "Always bothering your old head about someone's feelings! I do wish you would stop it! As for these children, I tell you, Michael, it is a matter of business. We are no longer young. We must prepare for the time when we can no longer stand on corners and in church doors and beg. My fingers even now are growing clumsy. Who will take care of us then if we do not train these children?"

"I suppose so," said Michael wistfully, "But it does seem a pity. You should have seen that chair."

"I've heard about it enough at any rate," said Martha. "You should have taken it. You could have sold it for a few kopeks.

"I couldn't," said Michael.

"All right," said Martha. "This is another matter; these

children. You heard what I said. Now here is what I plan. We will go to Lodz and there we will stay for the next year or two. This war cannot last forever, and when it is well past, why, then we will strike out in the world. I know little girls. These will both be beauties when they are a few years older." She laughed as she dragged Elinor along. "I tell you I did well when I picked up these pearls."

"No doubt; no doubt!" Michael answered. He could not but look with pity on the two children however. He was a man whose whole life had been evil, but somewhere in him was a spark of kindness and tenderness. He fought, he drank, he stole, he lied; but the sight of the two poor little girls dragging miserably along with the remorseless woman somehow touched his heart. He knew that he would often beat them, and he would also give them their first lessons in picking pockets; but he knew, too, that there would be times when he would shield them from the cold, relentless fury of the woman.

So it was with a feeling of pity for the weary little feet that he asked, "Where do we go tonight? I am tired."

"Tired?" scorned Martha. "You are ever tired! However, we will eat some supper, and then on to Lodz."

"Walk?" asked the other man, who had not spoken before.

"No," said Martha. "I have a pocketful of money. No, you don't," she added as the man came close to her. "Here's a handy knife if you try that. Something tells me to get out of here as soon as we can and it will take too long to walk with these burdens. Besides, they would never stand it. You may be sure I would not spend this money on the railroad if I could help myself.

She turned into a doorway. The house was deserted.

"Here," she said, "I will stay here with these two, while you get something for me to drink. Also go to the railroad and see if the trains are running. And hurry!"

She found a chair for herself, pushed the two children in the corner farthest from the door, and settled herself to wait, while the two men walked leisurely out of the house and away.

An hour later Michael hurried back. Martha greeted him sourly.

"Don't pretend to hurry, lazy one," she scolded. "I know where thou hast been. Did you bring what I asked?"

"I bring news," said Michael, glancing at the two children.

"Bah! That is dry drinking," said Martha, making a face. "Well, have it over!"

"There is a search on for the little one," said Michael. "I know who she is.

If they find her with us - " He drew his hand across his neck with the whistling sound of a knife.

"Who is she then?" asked Martha in astonishment.

Michael stooped and whispered in her ear.

"Ai! Ai!" exclaimed Martha. "No wonder her hands are delicate and small! Well, we have got to go on with it now. And quickly, too. How will we get out of here? Shall we trust the cars? Do they run? Answer, Michael, what did you find out?"

"A lot of things," said Michael. "First place, the station is watched, so I bought two tickets for Lodz. We men will go down there tomorrow."

"And leave me here!" asked Martha furiously.

"No, no, no!" said Michael. "Will you wait until I finish?

When I came from the railroad, I passed a great empty motor truck. Some soldiers are getting it ready to go to Lodz tonight. They are going for more munitions. It belongs to the enemy, but thanks to my German mother, I am German at will; so I spoke to them. I told them about my wife and two little children who were going to walk to Lodz. It was great luck. They said you could go with them.

"Think of that!" said Martha. "Not to walk a step, and to ride down that beautiful road in a truck. What a wonder! I never expected to get into one of those great horseless things. Well, what did you say then, stupid?"

"You are to go down now, and they will start soon. But they do not want the officers to know they are taking you. It is only because of my German and my nice way," he laughed. "Well, get up, and we will go over."

"I am almost afraid," said Martha.

"There is no way as good as this," the man assured her. "You will be safe. You will rest quite well under the canvases in the truck. And the road is indeed smooth."

He lifted Rika and led the way. It was growing late, and they hurried to the place near headquarters where the great track stood. Michael did not wait for anyone to come. He jumped in, and made a sort of nest in the canvas covers that were lying in the bottom. In this he seated Martha and the children, warning the woman to hold fast to the girls. Then he covered them cleverly with the lightest of the covers, saw that no one would guess that the truck was occupied, and proceeded to sit on the nearby curb and smoke. He was afraid that someone would throw something heavy in the truck, and bring a scream, from one of the children.

Presently the two soldiers who were to drive came out. They had had a good meal and were smoking contentedly. Michael went up to them. He opened his hand and showed three coins.

George Durston

"Here is all my wealth. I will share it with for your kindness to my wife and dear little ones," he said in a trembling voice.

The men shook their heads, but he insisted, and they took the offered coins, protesting that they would take their passengers safely to Lodz.

"Ah! What goodness!" said Michael with deep feeling. "If I could ever repay you!"

"That's all right," said one of the soldiers. "Just be silent about the load we are carrying. Tell no one. Our Captain is in the deuce of a temper. He would punish anything today." He drew on his gloves and mounted to his seat. The other soldier swung up beside him.

"It's a pity we can't take you too," said he; "but it wouldn't be safe. Good- bye."

"Good-bye," said Michael in a trembling voice. "Good-bye, wife! Good-bye, my sweet children!"

Martha pinched Elinor roughly. "Say goodbye!" she hissed, and a frightened little voice called, something that was almost lost in the sound of the engine as the car started. Martha stifled a shriek. This was a terrifying experience. As the car rolled onward, the two children, both accustomed to riding in motor cars, and too tired to mind the unyielding springs and hard tires of the truck, were lulled to sleep; but Martha sat wide-eyed, not daring to make the least outcry, and afraid to follow her heart's wish and jump to the ground. The night was filled with terrors, and when at dawn the car stopped, and a soldier brought her a can of coffee she was too stiff and frightened to speak.

When at last they reached Lodz, the two men were obliged to lift her to the ground. They set them down on the outskirts of the city and Martha hurried, as well as she could with her tired muscles, and the children dragging at her side, to the hovel where her sister lived.

There was a long talk then, and many explanations, and Martha rested and slept as though she never would rise again. When she did finally get up, she had lost all count of the time, but Michael was there, and the children were trying to get a handkerchief from the pocket of a coat suspended from the ceiling by a cord.

"Get it so carefully that you will not stir the coat, and you will have a piece of candy." The children tried again and again.

Martha groaned and disturbed them.

"Well, at last I am rested," she said. "Michael, thou fool, when next you get me such a place - " She groaned again.

"Better that than not at all, eh, Martha?" laughed the man.

"We might have walked it," she declared.

"Yes. In how many days, he demanded, "'with those children at heel?"

"Of course," she said, "but it was frightful." She shook her head. "We rocked and tossed like a ship at sea. And those children slept. Slept all the way. I could have beaten them!"

She turned to her sister. "You say you have no money? We will have to go and get some then." She turned to the children and studied them critically. "Those clothes won't do," she said. "Where is there a place where I can get them something else to wear?"

"Two houses down," said her sister. "I will go with you."

The women were not gone long, and came back with a bundle of children's clothing. Michael was still patiently teaching them the handkerchief trick, Rika's little face was puckered, and she was ready to cry although Michael had given her several pieces of candy. It did not take long to take off the clothes the children had been wearing, and dress them instead more in accordance with the parts they were to play.

Then Martha took a stick and stood before Elinor.

"Look at me!" she commanded, and when the child's frightened eyes sought her face she said, "You are to beg for your supper, do you hear? As soon as you see a kind looking lady or gentleman, you are to put out your hand, and say, 'Please, we are starving,' like that. Say it!"

Elinor was silent.

"Say it!" she repeated. But Elinor was still.

"Do you want to be beaten?" Martha asked in a terrible voice. "Do you?"

Elinor found her voice. "No," she said in Polish. "No, please do not beat me, but I cannot beg. My brother will come soon and get me. I do not want any supper. I will wait for him."

Martha sat down, the stick still in her hand, and thrust her ugly face close to the child's.

"Hear me!" she growled. "Your brother will never come for you. He is dead. Dead, I tell you! You will never see him again. You are going to live here with me, and you are going to do just what I tell you or I shall beat you so you will never forget it. Now do you understand?"

Elinor looked her steadily in the eyes.

"Yes," she said.

"Then say what I told you," said Martha, getting to her feet.

Elinor looked at her, then reading the threat in her eyes, she said, "Please, we are starving." It seemed more than her independent spirit could bear even with the fear of the stick on her heart. She added, "Some day I shall ran away."

"That settles it!" cried Martha. "We will settle this now!"

She threw the helpless child on the ground and began beating her with the stick. For a long while Elinor endured it, then unable to keep silent under the pain, she burst into screams and sobs. The woman continued her blows until Elinor's voice held a thin note of agony, and she lifted her and flung the quivering little body on a pile of rags, and sat herself down by the table.

"That ought to break her spirit," she said.

She waited until the sobs and cries subsided, and then called the child. The terrified little girl slipped from the bed and ran to her tormentor. Martha looked at her critically.

"That did you good," she said. "Now we will get out of here, and go to work."

"Have you any money at all?" asked her sister, turning to Michael.

"A little," he grudgingly admitted.

"Well, let us have enough to go to the market while it is open. I go late each morning, and buy the spoiled vegetables that are left over."

"A good plan," said Martha.

When they had finished with the market, the women walked slowly down through the city, begging wherever they could. They were able to recognize foreigners wherever they met them, although they were not many. Always, however, they gave, and gave generously. The store of coins in Martha's sack grew and grew.

"We will have to exchange this stuff for a few larger coins somewhere," she said. "I think we can do so safely at the railroad station. Let us go there."

The day had been a time of torture for the two children. Elinor was so tired that she thought that she would fall at each step, but the relentless hand held her up and pulled her on.

Rika, in the other woman's arms, had fallen asleep several times.

They did not mind that; her tear-stained little face with its long, curling lashes looked very pitiful, and as long as she slept they told a sad story, about her being lame. But Elinor had to walk; and she was sure that when she fell from exhaustion, Martha would probably kill her.

There was a great crowd at the station, and dozens of other beggars; but Martha noted with satisfaction that none had such beautiful children to beg for. There were many more coins in the sack before long, and just as Elinor's knees bent, under her, and she thought that now at last she would fall, the women set the children on a big box, and with the most horrible threats if they, stirred or spoke to anyone, walked off to the ticket office to change the small coins into something safer to handle.

CHAPTER XI

THE RED CROSS CAR

When Warren was dismissed from the hospital, he found himself being stared at by Ivan in a very perplexing manner. Finally he demanded the reason. Ivan laughed.

"You look so clean," he said. "Your face does not go with the rest of you, those ragged clothes and all that. Besides, I have not seen what your natural face looked like for a few days. I had forgotten just what you did look like."

Warren smiled.

"Just the same, it did seem good to clean up little," he said. "However, just to oblige you I'll put on a few frills." He stooped and rubbed his hands in some plaster dust, and transferred it to his face. Ivan studied the change.

"That's better," he said. "As long as we have to wear these clothes, I think we had better look the part. There is one thing certain though. We are dressed exactly as we were in Warsaw, when we were visiting our friends, the thieves. I wish we could get some other clothes."

"I hadn't thought of that," said Warren. "I wish we could change, but how can we?"

"I don't know," said Ivan. "Certainly we can't risk having

George Durston

those people see us. We will have to be cautious."

"Where shall we go, I wonder?" mused Warren.

"I don't suppose it matters now," said Ivan. "It is so late in the afternoon. Tomorrow morning we will have to watch the market. They will be sure to come for more provisions."

"True enough," said Warren. "Let's go down to the central station and see if the trains are running again."

The boys sauntered down through the streets without being molested by the sharp-eyed soldiers who patrolled the way. They found the station a busy place. The trains were once more running, on broken schedules of course, but everything was so nearly adjusted to the usual order that there was transportation for the hundreds who were eagerly seeking passage. There were a great many foreigners carefully clutching their transports and hurrying out of the country. At the back of the station stood an automobile, a low, racing roadster.

"We had a ride in her last night," said Warren, as he approached and recognized the machine. "And it was some ride, wasn't it, Ivan?"

"It certainly was," said Ivan, smiling. "What's the red cross flag on it I wonder?"

"The Princess has given it over to the hospital, I suppose," said Warren. "No one will stop it now. Wonder who drives it? I'm sorry for anyone who rides with the crazy guy who tried to run it last night. "

"Here is the chauffeur now," said Ivan, stepping back as a dark, burly man approached the machine and took a package from the tool-box.

"He is a new one," said Warren.

They wandered around the corner of the building and mingled with the throngs waiting for the train. It came puffing in, and as the crowd pressed forward, Warren heard a familiar, coarse, whining voice behind him. He looked; and as he did so, he was conscious of Ivan who, with the quickness of a bird, slipped between two people, and was out of sight. Instantly Warren followed him. They met behind a truck loaded with boxes.

Warren was shaking. "Did you see?" he asked.

"Yes," said Ivan in a low voice. "Elinor and Rika, too! What are we going to do?"

"I don't know," said Warren. "Just do what we have to do when the time comes. Don't risk them another hour. Elinor looks half dead. Keep out of sight and watch for a chance. Don't let the girls see you, any more than the women. They would give it away, sure. Come on!"

He slipped quickly through the crowd, only a boy, and unnoticed. Behind, at his heels, came a thin lad, soiled and ragged. It was Prince Ivan, Prince of one of the greatest houses in Warsaw, but his own father would not have recognized him. Together they slyly watched the two women in front of them who, each with a child, begged pitifully of the travelers. The woman who had Rika held her in her arms, but poor little Elinor, on foot, reached a tiny hand toward the passing throng, and fearfully glanced at her ugly jailer as she did so.

The train remained on the track. It was evidently going to make up a section. The women wandered here and there, and finally approached a big packing case near the station door. Here they stood, evidently consulting. One woman slyly, showed the other a handkerchief full of kopeks. Then while the boys scarcely dared to breathe, they seated the two children on the box, and with a fearful threat which caused the face of Elinor to turn even paler, they hurried into the waiting room, and turned towards the ticket window.

George Durston

"Now!" said Warren, "and be quick!"

He ran up to the children, and taking his sister in his arms, pressed his hand over her mouth until he had spoken a word in her ear. Then followed by Ivan carrying Rika, he walked steadily round the corner of the platform.

Before him stood the roadster, with the Red Cross flag. Without an instant's hesitation, he slipped into the driver's seat, Elinor still in his arms. He thrust her between his knees, as Ivan took the other seat, and tucked little Rika out of sight in the same manner.

As he did so, they heard a series of hoarse screams, and the two women, beating the air and wringing their hands, came rushing around the corner. Warren started the car full speed, and they started with a jerk that almost threw them out. Looking behind, Ivan saw the women point to the car and to his dismay a soldier on a motorcycle jumped from his machine and ran up to them. As the car sped down the long avenue, Ivan saw a last glimpse of the man returning to his machine. They were followed.

"They are after us!" he said to Warren.

"What with?" asked Warren, his eyes on the road. "There was no other machine."

"A soldier on a motorcycle. Make the first turn you can."

Warren whipped the little racer round one curve and then another. He was thinking deeply.

Elinor commenced to cry.

"Don't let them get me, Warry!" she begged.

"You are all right, dear," he answered. Then to Ivan:

"I have it. Didn't you say you knew that Princess what-is-her-name that owns this car?"

"Yes, a little," said Ivan.

"Well, you could make her recognize whose son you are, couldn't you?"

"Of course!" said Ivan.

"Well," said Warren, "we can't get anywhere with the car, and the only thing for us to do is to go to the hospital as quickly as we can, and you get hold of that Princess, and do some explaining. You see she stands in with both sides because of the hospital. It's her own sister's house, isn't it?"

"Yes," said Ivan, "and that's the only thing to do. This is a Red Cross car now, and there will be a big fuss about it."

"Where are we, anyway?" said Warren, slowing down to regulation speed.

"Turn to your left and ahead for three blocks, then once to the right, and you will see the palace in the distance," said Ivan.

They swept on, reached the marble steps of the building, stopped the car, and Warren leaped to the ground.

He looked at his little sister. He could not speak, but held out his arms, and she sprang into them. She clung to him trembling, and calling his name over and over while he pressed kisses on her pale little cheeks. With Ivan still holding Rika, they hurried up the steps just as the soldier on the motorcycle whirled to the curb.

He leaped from his seat and followed them, talking furiously in German, but the boys were so close to the open door that they slipped inside before the man could lay a hand on them. A nurse came up and a doctor, and the boys commenced, both

George Durston

at once, one in Polish and the other in English, to explain matters. The doctor looked grave. No one would dream that the two thin, pale, ragged little girls were anything but the beggars they looked to be, and the doctor shook his head.

Ivan stamped his foot. "I want the Princess!" he said. "She will straighten this out. Send someone for the Princess!" he demanded.

"I think she is out," said the nurse; "but I will send." She gave a message to an assistant, and they waited in silence while the girl was gone. She returned in a moment.

"The Princess is not here," she said, "but Madame, her sister, is coming." As she spoke, the door opened, and the lovely face of Princess Olga appeared.

"What is the trouble?" she asked of the doctor, and glanced at the group before her.

One low cry she gave; one spring, and little Rika was folded to her breast. The baby arms were close around her neck, the little face hidden while the Princess murmured loving names and strained the little form close to her heart.

Warren was the first to speak. He turned to Ivan.

"Well, what do you know about that?" he said solemnly in English.

The doctor turned to Ivan and plied him with questions.

Presently the Princess looked up.

"Who are you?" she asked, noting the pale child at his side.

"My name is Morris, Warren Morris," said Warren. He would have explained farther, but the Princess, rising, lifted her head and looking reverently up, said simply, "God is good! Come with me!" Imperiously she led the way down the great hall, now full of cots, and to a narrow door. She opened this and pushed Warren through ahead of her.

And Evelyn, poor heart-broken Evelyn, saw him as he came. Then she had him in her arms; and for once Warren could not kiss her enough or hug her hard enough. But he had to be shared with Elinor who commenced to look happy once more.

"Where is father?" asked Warren doubtfully, when Evelyn seemed assured that he was real, and that she actually had Elinor back again.

"Out with the Princess," said Evelyn. Then for the first time she noticed that the Princess was gone, and the door shut, and they were alone.

"Warren, you must be very good to father," said Evelyn gently. "He has suffered more than I ever knew anyone could. He takes all the blame for everything."

"Well, - " said Warren stubbornly, "a lot of it has been his fault."

"That doesn't matter now," said Evelyn. "Father is not to blame for the forgetfulness and selfishness in his work that we find so hard to bear. His parents are the ones to blame. They thought because he was such a bright child that everything should be made secondary to his needs. And then our dear mother went right on spoiling him. So now we, who are his children, can't expect to make him over. We have just got to remember that he is a truly great man - in his own line, and we are very proud of him. We are older now, and things won't be so hard for us."

"You bet we are older!" said Warren. "I don't expect to feel any older when I am ninety than I do now. But you are right about father. I have felt pretty sore, sis, I confess, and when I thought you were dead, and Elinor lost for good, it didn't seem as though I could forgive him. You are right about his people. Folks have no right to let a kid run the whole place like that, even if it is to develop his brain. I'll tell you one thing, if ever I have any kids of my own, I'm going to bring them up after a plan of my own."

Evelyn smiled. "I hope it will work, Warry," she said.

Warren looked savage. "It will, you can bet," he said. "I will make them go to school, of course, but they will begin to qualify for the Boy Scouts when they are about three years old; and they will learn to shoot, and know first aid when they are about four, and a lot of other things when they are five or so."

Evelyn groaned. "I'm sorry for those children, Warren," she laughed.

"Well, perhaps I will give them a little more time, but they have got to understand that efficiency is as necessary when they are sixteen as when they are sixty. Do you remember those chaps we saw in Switzerland? They were way up in their studies. You know I went to school with a fellow one day, but when school was out they were doing things worth while. And the fellow I knew had the dandiest rifle I ever saw. He said it was a prize from the government for target shooting. And he knew how to handle that gun, too. He said there was a fine for carelessness with firearms.

"Then these Germans. I've seen dozens of fellows no older than I am. They are hard as nails and fit every minute. Say, what's father going to do?" he demanded. "Are we going to spend our lives here, or are we going home?"

"Father does not know yet that you are here, you know," Evelyn reminded him. "He ought to be here soon now."

"Let's get him to go home as soon as we can," said Warren.

"I've seen about all I can stand of these horrors." He put his arm around Evelyn's shoulders and embraced both dear sisters.

"Evelyn, we will never be the same children again," he said sadly. "Oh, I'm homesick for America! I want to go home to Princeton. I want to have it come Fourth of July and hear the crackers go off and see the flag hanging out of store windows, and upside down and wrong side to on people's lawns the way they most always hang it. I want to hooray for 'Mericky.' I am dead, dead sick of this, sissy. I want to go where I belong."

"Poor old Warren!" said Evelyn. "I know how you feel. I want to go, too. But you can't shake the dust of Europe off like that, you know. We have made friends, good friends here, and you will have to keep in touch with the Polish Boy Scouts. You can't shirk that, you know."

"No, of course not," agreed Warren. "I just want to go home and soak up on America for awhile. I've got a lot of things to tell those fellows, too!" he said solemnly.

"Well, we could go right away if father is willing, and if we could get passports and transportation," said Evelyn. "Only I've got to go back and get the baby."

"The WHAT!" shouted Warren.

"Why, the baby," said Evelyn. "The baby you brought me; the one you brought me from its dead mother."

"Sure enough!" said Warren. "Well, where is it, anyway?"

"Back in Warsaw," said Evelyn. "I left it with the woman who lived in the corner house. When the soldiers took us away, she came out to see what the disturbance was, and she offered to keep the baby."

"A baby!" said Warren. "So you are going to take it home! Well, that does seem almost the last straw! You don't suppose your friend in Warsaw would like to keep it?"

"No, I don't," said Evelyn firmly. "That woman has six, and her husband was killed, and she is ruined. She will have hard enough work feeding her own. She is an angel to keep it so, long. We have dozens of relatives over home, and they are all going to have the privilege of helping to care for our little war baby. I shall name her for the Princess."

"All right," said Warren. He went to the window and looked out. "I wish father would come," he said. "Is Jack with him? Suppose I go and look for them?"

"You will stay right here," said Evelyn. "I don't want one of you out of my sight from now on. Jack is with father. They went out to go to the market. Father has been helping a lot here. He has given the hospital all sorts of things that were badly needed. The Princess will send him in as soon as she comes. Isn't it like a fairy tale to think that we had little Rika all the time?"

"I wish you would begin at the beginning and tell me all that happened after you were arrested," said Warren. "I have had such a lot of scraps."

"All right," said Evelyn. She looked down at the little sister in her arms. "See," she said, "she has gone to sleep. The darling is exhausted."

Warren looked grave. "She has had the worst experience of all," he said. "We won't know for a good while just what she has undergone. I would not want to question her. It will have to come out in bits. And I think the baby will be a good thing after all. It will help occupy Elinor's attention and make her forget. Yes, we have got to get out of here as soon as we can on her account. Now go on."

Evelyn cuddled the sleeping child more closely, and commencing at the moment when the soldiers broke down the door, she told her brother the thrilling and almost unbelievable story of their adventure. Finally she reached the end. Warren had made no comments, but the stern and anxious expression of his face betrayed his feelings. Evelyn paused.

"And to think that I was right on the other side of that door when you were crying yesterday! Poor little sister, I hope you will never, never have to cry for me again."

There was a sound of rapid steps at the door. It was flung open and Jack rushed in, closely followed by the Professor.

Trouble and danger and separation change our viewpoint. There had been a time not long past when Warren regarded any demonstration of affection as unmanly, but now he found himself in his father's arms and only too glad to be there.

CHAPTER XII

OVER THE SEA

Evelyn had told the truth. Professor Morris was a changed man. For the first time in all his orderly humdrum student existence, he had had to face war and death and murder, and all the crimes that stalk through a land at such times.

It had accomplished what all the arguments, all the lecturing, all the entreaties in the world would never have accomplished. Professor Morris had been shaken out of himself. There had been sleepless nights when his life had looked very poor and thin and useless. What was his book, a dry thing of many pages, when he compared it to the needs of the dear children who had been so loyal and so true to him? It came to him that culture may be made as selfish and as harmful as any vice there is.

But Benjamin Morris was, after all, a man; and late as it was, it was not too late for him to humbly resolve to be a better father, and a more valuable citizen. And he kept his word.

Presently Ivan returned. The boy had purposely kept away until the reunited family had had time to talk everything all over. When he entered, Professor Morris sat looking at him, with his eyes narrowed and a puzzled look on his face. Evelyn knew that look, and wondered what was passing in her father's mind. He sat quite silent, and after a little left the room. When he returned, he brought the Princess Olga, who was leading the little Rika as though she dared not leave her out of her sight.

"We have been talking things over," said Princess Olga. "Of course the only reasonable thing for Professor Morris to do is to return to America without delay. He has no right to remain here and possibly endanger the lives of so many young people, and there is nothing that he can do for us. Some day we will want help, and then we know that yon will all come to our aid. Ivan, we have been talking it all over with my husband, the Prince, and we have decided that the best thing for you to do is to go also. Wait," she said as Ivan shook his head. "My boy, our country is in ruins. Your father is at the front, we know not where. You can not serve him by remaining here where you are, every moment in danger of being arrested and held as a prisoner or worse. Your estates are in ruins; but not withstanding, you are, after your father, the head of your house. You owe to Poland the one thing you can now do for her. You must preserve and safeguard your life. And you must go to the University where Professor Morris is such an eminent instructor. You must learn statesmanship. Some day, Ivan, Poland will need you. What chance have you here now in this stricken land?

"I want you to go, Ivan. We will take the responsibility. And I want you to take these jewels, and use them for your expenses and education!" She held out a glittering handful of priceless gems.

"No," said Professor Morris firmly. "Princess, you will need all you have. It happens that I have plenty of money, and we live very simply, so there is enough and to spare for the two children we hope to take with us."

"Two?" said the Princess.

"The baby, " said the Professor. "I confess the needs of an infant seem too complex and difficult for me to cope with, but my daughter entertains no fears, and insists upon taking the little fellow with us."

"It's a girl, father," corrected Evelyn.

"Ah, yes," said the Professor, bowing. "I believe you did say that he is a girl."

"I have told him at least a dozen times," said Evelyn in a whisper to Warren.

"I suppose we have got to take her along, no matter what he is," Warren whispered back.

"However," said the Professor, glancing reprovingly at the children, "there is plenty of money, in reason, and if Ivan prefers, we will keep an account of his educational expenses, and at some future date he can repay what I shall deem necessary to expend for him."

"That is better," said the Princess. She turned to Ivan

"You will go, Ivan."

"Yes," said Ivan. Then sadly, "But I wish I could see my father."

"It is indeed hard," said the Princess. "We feel that he must be unhurt however, and I know that he will be so relieved, and glad to know that you are in a place of safety. So that is settled." She smiled.

"Now there is one more thing to be done. I have here a permit from the General in charge of the city. It gives us safe conduct on the roads to Warsaw and return, to get the baby. I have arranged for one of the nurses to go with the new chauffeur and Warren. I will take part of her duties, and Evelyn may assist me. She will get the baby and bring it here to us. They can go tonight, and return tomorrow. All will then be ready for your departure, if in the meantime Professor Morris can arrange to get your passports and your sailing privileges."

"It sounds easy," said Warren to Evelyn. "When do you suppose we will start?"

"As soon as the car is ready," said the Princess. "Get wraps for yourself, Warren. The nurse is ready, and she has everything needful for the baby."

"Oh, Warren, be careful, begged Evelyn. I declare I have half a mind to go with you!"

Warren laughed. "I have a whole mind that you will not!" he said, patting her shoulder. "You stay right here and don't go out of the place, and keep father and Ivan and Elinor where you can see them all the time. And if we are not back by noon tomorrow, don't begin to worry. Just lay our delay to a puncture or something of that sort. We won't be molested. The paper from the General is as good as a regiment of men. You had better believe that no one would dare hurt us, or even detain us while I have that to show them."

"Well, be careful just the same," begged Evelyn.

"I surely will," promised Warren.

Everything went as smoothly as Warren had anticipated. The trip to Warsaw was without a hitch. Again and again they were stopped by soldiers, and each time the paper from the Commanding General acted like magic. Indeed, they were more than once assisted on their way, or directed to short cuts. In Warsaw it was the same. Warren, however, avoided that part of the city where he thought he might come in contact with Captain Handel, and driving by another route, approached the house of the neighbor who had so kindly taken care of the homeless little waif. The child was safe and well, having suffered less than they had feared from its terrible experience. With a thousand thanks and promises to write, Warren left the good, motherly woman and started on the return trip.

They slept at an obscure little village that night in peace. The town had been overlooked in the tempest of war, and was untouched.

At the inn they found good food and plenty of it. In the morning, when they started, they found every available part of the car crammed with offerings for the wounded soldiers. The chauffeur had spent a busy evening talking to the horrified villagers and it is to be believed that the terrors he had witnessed in Lodz and elsewhere did not lose in the telling. So there were all sorts of offerings for the wounded; bread and dried fish and cheese; and money, sometimes gold, sometimes a single kopek wrapped in scraps of paper, written over with heartfelt prayers of pity. There was scarcely room for the passengers to crowd in the car.

Warren took the wheel, and the chauffeur, still the hero of the occasion, stood on the running board and waved his cap and called his farewells as long as they were in sight.

The baby slept most of the time. It was a good baby, and Warren began to regard it with less distrust. They reached Lodz without accident and as they drew up at the palace, now only a hospital, Warren's watch stood at twelve. It had been a wonderful trip.

Everything was going well. The Prince was stronger, and his wife, the beautiful Princess, was smiling happily.

All that day and the next the Professor and the three boys went from office to office and back again to the army headquarters, getting the necessary papers.

It was a difficult matter to get everything adjusted, but finally it was done, and there was no longer any reason for them to remain.

They said good-bye to the Princess and her children, and at last started on the journey home.

It was a time to be remembered as long as they lived. All of Europe was plunged in gloom. Even the neutral countries they touched or crossed in their roundabout way were oppressed by such sorrow that it was almost as bad as war.

Reaching a seaport at last, they secured passage on a slow American boat, and it was not until they watched the shore receding from their view that they actually believed that they were on the way home.

"Just the things we have seen coming over from Lodz would fill a book," said Warren to the group at the rail.

"I wouldn't want to read it," said Jack, shuddering.

"Nor I!" said Evelyn. "Oh, boys, you don't know how funny you look in the clothes you have on!"

"What's the matter with my clothes?" said Warren, looking down at the very short trousers and very long coat he was wearing. "I don't see but what I am all right, but doesn't Jack look cuty-cute? Kind of Lord Fauntleroy effect!"

Everyone stared at Jack, who looked himself over in surprise. "It is all they had at that store we went to that would fit me. I try to turn those pants up, but they keep coming down." Everyone laughed as Jack stooped and once more tried to turn up the loose trousers which enveloped his slim legs. Left to themselves, they reached half way to his ankles, so Jack, who was used to knickerbockers, had carefully rolled them to his knee. The result was that most of the time one leg or the other hung dismally down its full length. His jacket was a short roundabout, something like an Eton jacket, and his shirt was soft and frilled.

"I don't see why we didn't just wear the things we had on,"

he complained.

"I guess not!" said Warren. "Those work clothes? Why, Jack, see how dressy we are now! We look like somebody; a bunch of 'em! We have got sample clothes from half the countries in Europe. See how neutral that makes us! Take yourself, Jack. Your feet are Polish, and your pants are German, and the top of you looks Dutch. Is it?"

"My cap came from home," said Jack furiously, "and so did my face! The minute we get out here a way, I am going to yell Hurrah for America as loud as ever I can."

"Wow!" said Warren. "Excuse me, Jack, old fellow, I didn't mean to be disrespectful. We are all in the same fix as far as clothes go. Even Evelyn looks a little queer. 'All the world is a little queer,' he quoted, 'and thee is a little queer.'"

Safe on board ship, our party found that they were utterly tired out. They slept hour after hour; they were furiously hungry. The days went swiftly, without accident. Professor Morris, true to his new resolutions, spent a great part of each day with his children, and they found him a most delightful and amusing companion. He developed an alarming fondness for the baby, which he persisted in calling "him." He was fond of holding the quiet little creature, but after one of his lapses into the forgetfulness of the past, he happened to think of something he wanted to do so he laid his newspaper in Evelyn's lap, and before she could stop him placed the baby firmly in a waste paper box head down.

After that Evelyn watched him. They had brought a young refugee with them as nurse for the baby, so Evelyn was not burdened with too much care.

The boys played games and made plans and wrote letters. Ivan commenced a diary. He said he would never be able to remember every single thing that was happening, and going to happen, and he didn't want to forget it. Warren planned to have an evening with the home Scouts and tell them all that had occurred.

"And you will be Exhibit A," he declared, clapping Ivan on the shoulder.

The voyage drew to an end, as all fortunate voyages will. The last night came clear and fine. There was a stir of joyful anticipation on the great ship. Everybody packed up what trifles they had been able to bring away with them. Everybody talked and exchanged addresses and said good-bye. The day of landing is always too, full and confused for anything of that sort. Once more the Professor's manuscript seemed to him to be a thing of value. He picked it up and put it down a thousand times. It was a relief to everyone when the hour grew so late that even the most restless turned in, and went to sleep or at least tried to.

At gray dawn Ivan was aroused by Warren shaking him.

"Get up, Ivan, get up!" he cried. "I can see it!" The boy was shaking violently, and his teeth chattered.

"What ails you?" said Ivan, speaking in Polish. "See what?"

Warren answered in English. "America. Home, the little old United States!" A dry sob choked him. "Oh!" he said, "I didn't know I felt like this! Hurry up, old Scout! Dress and let's get out!"

Voices sounded through the ship; people stirred and hurried with their dressing. It was as though a shock of electricity had stirred them. Certainly there had been no spoken call.

As the boys hurried to the deck, the risen sun, a ball of gold, blazed like a celestial blessing, a flood of glory on the marvelous shore line ahead. Warren rushed forward.

But Ivan, without a look, turned and made his solitary way to the stern of the ship, and there, all alone, looked away over the empty sea.

For long he gazed. His eyes were filled with tears.

"Good-bye, my father," he said. "Good-bye, my country. I will come back to you." He flung his hand out in a passionate gesture of farewell. Then with a last look, Prince Ivan, homeless, countryless, and fatherless, slowly turned, and, the boy Ivan went soberly to join Warren, who, crazy with joy, hung yelling over the rail at the prow.

Before them, like the vision of an enchanted land, rose the wonderful shore line of the harbor; and before them, nearer and nearer, clearer and clearer, the Statue of Liberty, wise, strong, majestic, with the only true majesty of earth on her beautiful brow, the majesty of Freedom and of Truth.

They had reached America.

Choose from Thousands of 1stWorldLibrary Classics By

Adolphus WilliamWard
Aesop
Agatha Christie
Alexander Aaronsohn
Alexander Kielland
Alexandre Dumas
Alfred Gatty
Alfred Ollivant
Alice Duer Miller
Alice Turner Curtis
Alice Dunbar
Ambrose Bierce
Amelia E. Barr
Andrew Lang
Andrew McFarland Davis
Anna Sewell
Annie Besant
Annie Hamilton Donnell
Annie Payson Call
Anton Chekhov
Arnold Bennett
Arthur Conan Doyle
Arthur Ransome
Atticus
B. M. Bower
Basil King
Bayard Taylor
Ben Macomber
Booth Tarkington
Bram Stoker
C. Collodi
C. E. Orr
C. M. Ingleby
Carolyn Wells
Catherine Parr Traill
Charles A. Eastman
Charles Dickens
Charles Dudley Warner
Charles Farrar Browne
Charles Ives
Charles Kingsley
Charles Lathrop Pack
Charles Whibley
Charles Willing Beale
Charlotte M. Braeme
Charlotte M.Yonge
Clair W. Hayes
Clarence Day Jr.
Clarence E. Mulford

Clemence Housman
Confucius
Cornelis DeWitt Wilcox
Cyril Burleigh
D. H. Lawrence
Daniel Defoe
David Garnett
Don Carlos Janes
Donald Keyhole
Dorothy Kilner
Dougan Clark
E. Nesbit
E.P.Roe
E. Phillips Oppenheim
Edgar Allan Poe
Edgar Rice Burroughs
Edith Wharton
Edward J. O'Biren
John Cournos
Edwin L. Arnold
Eleanor Atkins
Elizabeth Cleghorn
Gaskell
Elizabeth Von Arnim
Ellem Key
Emily Dickinson
Erasmus W. Jones
Ernie Howard Pie
Ethel Turner
Ethel Watts Mumford
Eugenie Foa
Eugene Wood
Evelyn Everett-Green
Everard Cotes
F. J. Cross
Federick Austin Ogg
Ferdinand Ossendowski
Francis Bacon
Francis Darwin
Frances Hodgson Burnett
Frank Gee Patchin
Frank Harris
Frank Jewett Mather
Frank L. Packard
Frederick Trevor Hill
Frederick Winslow Taylor
Friedrich Kerst
Friedrich Nietzsche
Fyodor Dostoyevsky

Gabrielle E. Jackson
Garrett P. Serviss
Gaston Leroux
George Ade
Geroge Bernard Shaw
George Ebers
George Eliot
George MacDonald
George Orwell
George Tucker
George W. Cable
George Wharton James
Gertrude Atherton
Grace E. King
Grant Allen
Guillermo A. Sherwell
Gulielma Zollinger
Gustav Flaubert
H. A. Cody
H. B. Irving
H. G. Wells
H. H. Munro
H. Irving Hancock
H. Rider Haggard
H. W. C. Davis
Hamilton Wright Mabie
Hans Christian Andersen
Harold Avery
Harold McGrath
Harriet Beecher Stowe
Harry Houidini
Helent Hunt Jackson
Helen Nicolay
Hendy David Thoreau
Henrik Ibsen
Henry Adams
Henry Ford
Henry Frost
Henry James
Henry Jones Ford
Henry Seton Merriman
Henry Wadsworth
Longfellow
Henry W Longfellow
Herbert A. Giles
Herbert N. Casson
Herman Hesse
Homer
Honore De Balzac

Horace Walpole
Horatio Alger, Jr.
Howard Pyle
Howard R. Garis
Hugh Lofting
Hugh Walpole
Humphry Ward
Ian Maclaren
Israel Abrahams
J.G.Austin
J. Henri Fabre
J. M. Barrie
J. Macdonald Oxley
J. S. Knowles
J. Storer Clouston
Jack London
Jacob Abbott
James Allen
James Lane Allen
James Andrews
James Baldwin
James DeMille
James Joyce
James Oliver Curwood
James Oppenheim
James Otis
Jane Austen
Jens Peter Jacobsen
Jerome K. Jerome
John Burroughs
John F. Kennedy
John Gay
John Glasworthy
John Habberton
John Joy Bell
John Milton
John Philip Sousa
Jonathan Swift
Joseph Carey
Joseph Conrad
Joseph Jacobs
Julian Hawthrone
Julies Vernes
Justin Huntly McCarthy
Kakuzo Okakura
Kenneth Grahame
Kate Langley Bosher
L. A. Abbot
L. T. Meade
L. Frank Baum
Laura Lee Hope

Laurence Housman
Leo Tolstoy
Leonid Andreyev
Lewis Carroll
Lilian Bell
Lloyd Osbourne
Louis Tracy
Louisa May Alcott
Lucy Fitch Perkins
Lucy Maud Montgomery
Lydia Miller Middleton
Lyndon Orr
M. H. Adams
Margaret E. Sangster
Margaret Vandercook
Maria Edgeworth
Maria Thompson Daviess
Mariano Azuela
Marion Polk Angellotti
Mark Overton
Mark Twain
Mary Austin
Mary Cole
Mary Rowlandson
Mary Wollstonecraft
Shelley
Max Beerbohm
Myra Kelly
Nathaniel Hawthrone
O. F. Walton
Oscar Wilde
Owen Johnson
P.G.Wodehouse
Paul and Mable Thorn
Paul G. Tomlinson
Paul Severing
Peter B. Kyne
Plato
R. Derby Holmes
R. L. Stevenson
Rabindranath Tagore
Rahul Alvares
Ralph Waldo Emmerson
Rene Descartes
Rex E. Beach
Richard Harding Davis
Richard Jefferies
Robert Barr
Robert Frost
Robert Gordon Anderson
Robert L. Drake

Robert Lansing
Robert Michael Ballantyne
Robert W. Chambers
Rosa Nouchette Carey
Ross Kay
Rudyard Kipling
Samuel B. Allison
Samuel Hopkins Adams
Sarah Bernhardt
Selma Lagerlof
Sherwood Anderson
Sigmund Freud
Standish O'Grady
Stanley Weyman
Stella Benson
Stephen Crane
Stewart Edward White
Stijn Streuvels
Swami Abhedananda
Swami Parmananda
T. S. Ackland
The Princess Der Ling
Thomas A. Janvier
Thomas A Kempis
Thomas Anderton
Thomas Bailey Aldrich
Thomas Bulfinch
Thomas De Quincey
Thomas H. Huxley
Thomas Hardy
Thomas More
Thornton W. Burgess
U. S. Grant
Valentine Williams
Victor Appleton
Virginia Woolf
Walter Scott
Washington Irving
Wilbur Lawton
Wilkie Collins
Willa Cather
Willard F. Baker
William Makepeace
Thackeray
William W. Walter
Winston Churchill
Yei Theodora Ozaki
Young E. Allison
Zane Grey